NODDING'S CHRISTMAS

and other stories

JAMES O. WEEKS

author of

NODDING'S PEOPLE

Nodding's Christmas and other stories
© 2025 James O. Weeks

Cover design: Rebekah Wetmore
Editor: Andrew Wetmore

ISBN: 978-1-997827-03-0
First edition November, 2025

Moose House Publications
2475 Perotte Road
Annapolis County, NS B0S 1A0
moosehousepress.com
info@moosehousepress.com

Moose House Publications recognizes the support of the Province of Nova Scotia. We are pleased to work in partnership with the Department of Communities, Culture and Heritage to develop and promote our cultural resources for all Nova Scotians.

We live and work in Mi'kma'ki, the ancestral and unceded territory of the Mi'kmaw people. This territory is covered by the "Treaties of Peace and Friendship" which Mi'kmaw and Wolastoqiyik (Maliseet) people first signed with the British Crown in 1725. The treaties did not deal with surrender of lands and resources but in fact recognized Mi'kmaq and Wolastoqiyik (Maliseet) title and established the rules for what was to be an ongoing relationship between nations. We are all Treaty people.

Also by James O. Weeks

Nodding's People (available from Moose House)

The story "Drive thru Christmas" first appeared in the Moose House anthology *Blink and You'll Miss It*.

Foreword

David Nodding was a passive, lonely young man when he first encountered his "people"[1] and by comparison, they were caricatures. But after a summer at Stillwaters, he has grown into a happy and confident young man. His "people" have also rounded into caring characters. In *Nodding's Christmas* they determine what lies ahead.

"Wyatt Retired" is almost historically accurate. Wyatt Earp retired to California, owned a small mine, and spent visits to Los Angeles advising Tom Mix, John Ford, and a young John Wayne for their movies. He admired William S. Hart's deluxe Packard, but never learned to drive.

"Lurton Chestnut" is named after two guides in Utah's rugged Capital Reef, Clarence Chestnut and Lurt Knee. Both loved the harsh wilderness and spent their lives introducing it to "flatlanders." They would have admired the Chestnut Kid.

The Christmas season in Nova Scotia can be magical but also emotionally charged. The two young men in the holiday stories reflect the extremes.

JOW
September, 2025

---

1   In *Nodding's People*

As always, for Anne

Nodding's Christmas and other stories

Nodding's Christmas

1: Wild news

Emma Mitchell could scarcely believe her eyes. But there it was, clear as can be, on the news from Halifax. A great white shark off the coast of Liverpool!

Now, reports of tagged sharks were common during the summer. But this was a visual sighting by the crew of a lobster boat in December. The water was too cold, plain and simple.

So the sighting might have fooled the folks on the lobster boat, but the scientists who tracked the summer sharks wouldn't be so gullible. If and when the news reached them down in North Carolina or wherever they lived, they'd laugh it off as a joke by some drunk Canadian lobstermen.

Emma knew better. She had an apartment just on the edge of Lunenburg, and she kept up with the fleet during lobster season. The boat involved was handled by an all-female crew. Emma had met the captain last summer, so she knew this was not a party boat. If the crew reported seeing a shark, they saw what they believed was a shark.

Only a few people were aware of the truth, and Emma wasn't sure they could all be trusted. But she thought of one woman she believed she could notify. They both were part of a breakfast chat group that met every month. They were all aware of the local buffoons, but they kept up to date on conspiracies, too.

She sat down at her card table and peered at her phone, then tapped her friend's number. It rang once before her friend answered.

"Did you see it, Anne Marie? Just like I've been telling you. It shouldn't be anywhere near us, but there it was!"

"I saw it, Emma. So now what?"

"Now I go further down the South Shore and start digging. It's time to make this story public. There are nice places to stay in Liverpool until I have proof. Do you want to come along?"

"But you don't have a car, Emma."

"I've got the Harley Trike in Minnie's garage and an extra helmet. We can ride together, as long as it doesn't snow."

"Nonsense! You'd freeze your ears off, or slide right off the 103. We'll take my Buick, and besides, I have friends in Port Medway where we can stay.. They run a retreat, and I have a little apartment reserved for my visits."

"We need to get down there right away quick!" Emma said. "You can drive your Buick with our suitcases, but I'm in the mood for a ride on the Harley. I can stay warm in my road leathers. When can we go?"

"First thing after lunch," Anne Marie said. "I'll email them tonight so they're expecting us. By the way, the Buick has plenty of room. You can leave the motorcycle here."

"I feel better when I ride," Emma said. "I may be sixty-four, but I've been riding since I was twenty. It's where I feel free."

"I didn't realize that."

"I bet you didn't know about my tattoos, either," Emma said. "I keep them covered mostly now. Folks don't expect a senior citizen to have been a member of a cycle club."

"You don't show any signs of that.".

"When I lived out in Revelstoke, I rode with a lesbian gang. We were pretty hard core, don't you know."

"I didn't know you were—"

"I'm not," Emma said. "But coed cycle groups weren't for me. Too wild and woolly."

"I would have never guessed," Anne Marie said. "I'll hang up now and let my friends know we're coming."

"Don't tell them about the creatures just yet."

"The secret is safe with me."

Anne Marie hung up and went to find her suitcase.

2: Quiet Medway?

Port Medway is a small coastal village on the Atlantic coast of Nova Scotia. A couple of small general stores and an antique shop survive, but the largest store is Hagan's Haven, a private liquor store covering a territory not serviced by NSLC locations. Formerly Nipper's, the store is half owned by Chester Hagan, who also owns the large religious retreat down the road, Stillwaters.

Hagan is the owner, but he has hired two men to manage the operation. David Nodding, a hospitality graduate from Halifax, handles the lodging and food side of the retreat. The large main building houses offices and a chapel. The second floor features the main dining room, a smaller dining room, and a well-equipped kitchen.

On the top floor are apartments. One facing the coast houses Nodding. Kenzie Pearce and her young son, Wyatt, live across the hall from him. A third twin-bed guest apartment is reserved for Mrs. Saks, who spends summer months at Stillwaters.

Belpre Tobias is a former truck driver who runs the religious program. He and his family live in a house on the property. Next to his house and adjoining the main lodge is a two-story motel unit, which is fully occupied all summer.

In the off season, Stillwaters offers weekend or holiday programs. Christmas is celebrated with fine dining, festive decorations, and numerous religious services.

Toby was in the kitchen, making himself a sandwich, while Nodding cleaned an oven. He watched Toby scoop egg salad onto a slice of sourdough bread.

"I brought over a jar of olives from the house," Toby said. "I chop them in half and add them to my sandwich. Ever try egg and olive?"

"Not yet," Nodding said. "But if you leave the jar open I will in a minute."

"My mother always added olives to egg salad. but only the stuffed green ones. Not those brown ones. I never tried it with them."

"I can't imagine they'd be as good," Nodding said, standing up and closing the oven.

"Mom made great sandwiches." Toby spread the egg salad on the bread. "My favourite was when she buttered potato bread and then spread brown sugar on it. Darn, that is special eating."

"I don't think I'll try that one."

"The main reason I came over for lunch wasn't the egg salad," Toby said. "Hagan called me this morning. He's inviting Moses, you, and me to take a road trip up to Cape Breton for a couple of days. He'll meet us there."

"We've got to get ready for the Christmas guests. Though I guess I've placed the major orders already."

"Kenzie can handle reservations. Jean said she'll decorate the chapel, and Virginia will handle the rest of the decorations."

"The heat's off in the motel rooms," Nodding said.

"It's still early enough. Besides, Moses probably won't come with us. Hagan predicted he'll say no when he called me. He said Moses is a homebody and will want to get the heat and water running himself. But there's a bigger reason for you and me to accept."

"He's our boss." Nodding bit into his sandwich. "He's our friend, but he's still the boss."

"Right," Toby said. "You like the egg and olive?"

"I do. But I'm not going to try the brown sugar."

"I call it the Cindy Special,. She only made it on special occasions. My grandmother had a sandwich I called the Mimi Special. Ham and cheddar, grilled."

"Now that one I've tried."

"You have to spread mayo on the cheese and yellow mustard on the ham before you fry it up," Toby said. "The finished sandwich is some good."

"By the way," Nodding said. "We got a message last night from Mrs. Saks. She's arriving this afternoon with a friend. Virginia's up there now, making up the second bed and cranking up the heat."

"There we go. The good Lord just gave us a reason to drive up to Cape Breton tomorrow."

"Oh, she's not that bad."

"She's a sweet woman, I agree. But when she's around, there's trouble."

"That's all behind us," Nodding said. "Anyway, I'm making pot roast tonight, since they'll be here. Will you all be over?"

"For pot roast? You bet. I'll call Jean and tell her. She'll bring Christmas cookies for dessert."

Toby looked up as a middle-aged woman bustled into the kitchen. "Hey, Virginia."

"The apartment is made up and should be toasty when they get here." She was wearing her winter jacket, so it must have been brisk in the apartment.

"I'm doing a pot roast for supper," Nodding said. "Would you and Moses care to join us?"

"Don't you be telling Moses, else he'd want to come," Virginia said. "I'm trying a new recipe for stuffed peppers with vegetable protein instead of beef in them. He promised me he'd give them a real try. But thanks for inviting us."

"You folks are always welcome," Toby said

"We appreciate it," Virginia said. "I took care of that problem, Mr.

Dave. See you all tomorrow, before your trip, now."

"Will Moses be joining us?" Nodding asked.

"Oh, no. He says there's too much to be done here. But I told him he could join us women and kids for dinner. One night we're ordering pizza. We'll invite Ms. Saks and her friend, if they're interested. I'll catch you all later. Downstairs needs a good dusting."

She gave a wave and headed through the dining room to the stairs to the lobby.

"What problem was Virginia fixing?" said Toby.

"Mrs. Saks left a pistol taped under her bathroom sink," Nodding said. "We thought it might cause problems."

"Lordy, yes. Thanks for handling it. And at least Moses will be here if there are any problems."

"Oh, Jean and Kenzie can keep it under control. And Virginia, too."

3: Dinner guests

Mrs. Saks and her friend Emma arrived that afternoon and settled into the small apartment. They accepted Nodding's dinner invitation and came downstairs at six.

Nodding had set a large table in the dining room for the meal.

"I simply love pot roast," Emma said. "This is a treat. I live alone and never bother to cook a roast for myself."

"I do my grocery shopping in Bridgewater once every week," Mrs. Saks said. "So every month I go to the diner and enjoy meatloaf for dinner."

"Let's give thanks and enjoy this fine meal," Toby said.

The children bowed their heads but watched him. The room grew quiet. Nodding saw Toby smile slightly.

"Give us grateful hearts, dear Lord, for all your blessings, and make us ever needful of the minds of others."

He looked up. "I met a fellow once down in the Boston states who said the blessing that way. He was an educated fella, name of Hewett. He was a school teacher but drove bus in his summer break."

He took the meat platter and passed it along to the guests.

"What brings you down this way?" Toby's wife, Jean, said. "Not much is happening in Port Medway."

"Oh, but there is," Mrs. Saks said. "I'll let Emma explain."

Emma swallowed and glanced around the table. "I'm sure you've heard about the shark sightings off shore," she said.

"It was on the news," Jean said. "Very unusual for winter."

"Right you are," Emma said. "The water is too cold. So what they saw can't be sharks."

"Then what did they see?" Kenzie said. The table was quiet as everyone looked at Emma.

"Moonmen," she said. "They've come back to the South Shore."

"All the way from the moon?" Jean said. She frowned at Kenzie's son, Wyatt, who giggled.

"Maybe even further," Emma said. "They could be the same aliens who crashed near Shag Harbor years back. But wherever they come from, they're right out in the water. They might even have a secret base out there."

"Cool," Wyatt said. "Can we see them?"

"We hope so," Mrs. Saks said. "We know of a couple of men in Liverpool who own a boat. Emma wants us to hire them to take us out for a search."

"Good for you," Jean said. "Most of the boats are busy now that it's lobster season."

"I wondered about that," Mrs. Saks said. "But Emma got these names from a friend in Lunenburg. We made a date to meet them for coffee tomorrow."

"Speaking of tomorrow, I'd better get the kids home and ready for bed. We still have a week of school before Christmas break," Jean said.

"Can I go out on the boat with you?" Wyatt asked, ignoring Kenzie's frown.

"Not at first," Emma said. "We don't know if the moonmen are friendly, or even where they are. And remember, this whole business is a big secret for now. We don't want all kinds of gawking people out there scaring them away."

She smiled at Nodding. "Thank you so much for dinner." She grabbed one more cookie as she and Mrs. Saks stood up.

"You two behave, now," said Toby. "Dave and I will be away for a couple of days. We probably won't see you before we leave."

"We've got the dishes," Nodding said. "You folks have a pleasant evening." He smiled as the children jumped to their feet.

He and Toby carried the dishes to the kitchen as the guests went to the elevator. Jean, Kenzie, and their children used the stairs. The dining room was quiet within minutes.

As Nodding loaded the dishwasher, Toby leaned out to be certain the dining room was empty.

"Does that plan to charter a boat sound risky to you, too?"

"I thought I was being too suspicious," Nodding said. "I'll ask Moses to keep an eye on things. Those guys could make more money from a boatload of lobster than from a charter."

"It just don't feel right," Toby said. "Anyhow, let's leave early and grab some breakfast in Bridgewater. The diner stop is on me."

4: On the road

Moses came to work at seven, just in time to chat with Toby and Nodding. He agreed to keep an eye on Mrs. Saks and Emma.

"I don't think they have any idea what they'll experience out on the water," Moses said. "It's gonna be brutal with that cold wind."

He shook his head and went inside.

"At least your Subaru heat works," Toby said as they pulled out. "It'd be a frosty trip without it. By the way, I want to ask a favour."

"Sure."

"I brought Jesus along to watch over us."

Toby paused for a moment to see Nodding's reaction. When there was none, he relaxed. He pulled the small plastic figure out of his coat pocket and slid it up under the visor. "I plan to glue this one on my truck dashboard. My old one is cracked and leaning to the right." He looked over at Nodding.

"That's fine," Nodding said. He glanced up at the figure staring down at him, then back at the road. "Any idea about breakfast?"

"I feel like their special breakfast, the one with baked beans, a real Nova Scotia tradition. It's tasty enough to hold body and soul together. You? They have steak and eggs."

"I think I'll go for a cheese omelette with sausage. That should clog an artery or two. And a couple cups of coffee to keep me awake during the drive."

The diner would have a line later on, but there would be empty tables this early.

They settled into silently watching the road until they reached Bridgewater and the diner. They chose an empty booth instead of the counter, and coffee arrived with their menus. Toby ordered his breakfast with beans, while Nodding added green peppers to his omelette.

After a warm breakfast, Nodding drove back to the 103 while Toby searched for Christmas carols on the radio.

"I guess I'm a mite early," he said. "But the dang stores put out their displays on Remembrance Day. I should have brought my Hank Snow CD. Oh, well. I really think them old Christmas songs are the ones I look forward to most."

He gave up on the radio and they rode in silence up to the 102 and headed for Truro. The traffic was light, and soon they made the turn toward Cape Breton.

Finally, Toby sat up and turned to face Nodding. "What I'm gonna say is none of my business, but I'm gonna ask anyway. You ever hear from that girl with the jealous boyfriend?"

"She emailed me during the summer," Nodding said. "But I didn't answer. That's all in the past and it'll stay there. I've moved on with my life."

"Jean and I were talking about it, and I feel I gotta ask if your intentions with Kenzie were honourable."

"What do you mean, exactly?"

"You two have been seeing each other since summer. Jean and I care a lot about Kenzie, and we don't want her to get hurt. She had a rough enough time when her ex-husband left her."

"I don't honestly know where our relationship is headed," Nodding said. "But I will never do anything to hurt Kenzie."

"I'm sorry, Dave, but I had to ask."

"You asked because you're protecting her as a good friend. I respect that."

"Good," Toby said. "End of discussion. Now, exactly where on

Cape Breton are we going? I read the email before I gave it to you, but I've never explored that part of the province."

"It's beautiful in summer, when you can drive all the way up. But winters are rugged. We're headed just beyond Mabou, and so far there's only a dusting of snow. There's a distillery that has an inn and restaurant during summer, but somehow Hagan has arranged for them to have some rooms and meals for us. I've never been inside, but I've driven past. It's a spectacular area."

"Money can arrange a lot. It's a nice idea, but I still don't really know why we're invited. I guess we'll find out this evening."

Toby leaned back in his seat, glanced up at Jesus, and dozed off.

~

"Time for a break," Nodding said, turning off the car.

"What are we doing here?" Toby said, looking out at the Truro truck stop. "Haven't been here in almost a year. Golly."

"Jean asked me to stop here for a break. She said you were missing your pie and ice cream."

"I guess I am," Toby said, smiling up at the visor. "Let's go in, I'm buying. It feels like a lifetime since I was here. I'm living a different life these days. Praise the Lord."

"Glory be," a waitress behind the counter said. "Look who wandered in. I've missed you, Preacher."

"I've been working on the South Shore," Toby said. "But my buddy Dave and I couldn't pass up a chance to stop in. Haven't seen you in almost a year, Lena."

"Grab a stool, boys. Apple pie right out of the oven?" She ran a sponge over the counter, then took out a pen and her order tablet.

"Sounds perfect," Nodding said. "With coffee, please."

"Coffee's on the house for the holidays," Lena said. "It's getting to be just like old times. Your buddy Hagan come in with his wife two days ago. Say, is he doing okay?"

"Far as I know," Toby said. "Been a couple of weeks since I seen him. Why?" He frowned and looked up at Lena.

"You know how he'd come in and order potatoes and stuffing with gravy? The other day he just ordered chicken soup and only finished part of it. Not like the Hagan who used to drive those explosive tractors. Be right back with your pie."

"Might be because Lucille was with him," Nodding said.

"We can ask him at dinner," Toby said. "Here comes the pie!"

After their pie and coffee, Nodding talked Toby out of a pie for the road, and soon they were back on the highway. Nodding turned north after Truro, and they passed by his old town of Antigonish while Toby snoozed. He could see the university and realized he didn't miss the cafeteria at all. He had grown beyond it. Toby was still asleep, so he didn't say anything.

Toby woke up when they crossed the causeway into Cape Breton. "My cousin lives up here near Baddeck. Right up the road from the Alexander Graham Bell Museum. I should bring the family up to see him."

"Before we get busy in the spring might work," Nodding said.

"I'll think about it. Thing is, he's a bit weird. A couple of years ago he took to lining his baseball cap with tin foil to keep cosmic rays from frying his brain. He's a swell guy, but that kinda makes you wonder."

"I can see why. I'm taking the coastal route up through Judique so we won't go through Baddeck, if that's okay."

"Judique has that Celtic music centre," Toby said. "I hear that place is worth bringing the kids to. And nobody is wearing tin foil, neither. Their lunch room serves up a decent lobster roll, from what other drivers said."

"I'll have to come check it out," Nodding said. "I bet Kenzie would enjoy a little road trip."

He glanced over, but Toby was innocently looking out the window. Nodding smiled, realizing Toby was right. It was worth a visit.

They rode in silence through Judique and soon passed through Mabou, where Toby pointed out the Red Shoe Pub, now closed for the winter.

"When you get up this way, you gotta eat there. Their chowder or their meatloaf are worth getting. It's some good."

"I looked up the distillery dining room," Nodding said. "It sounds pretty good, too."

"Hagan likes good food. Looking forward to trying it."

Fifteen minutes beyond Mabou, they arrived at the distillery and inn. At check-in they were each given a room and told Hagan would meet them in the dining room in a half hour.

Nodding hoped Hagan would explain the reason for this conference so close to the holidays. And, it dawned on him, Hagan's wife Lucille didn't appear to be at the inn.

He carried his bag upstairs to a warm, comfortable room, washed up, and headed down to the dining room.

5: Rent-A-Boat

Mrs. Saks slowed her Buick as they crossed the bridge into Liverpool. Both women peered out at the lobster boat, alone at the dock.

"It looks solid enough," Emma said. "But I'll still wear a life vest to be on the safe side."

"If we end up in the water, we'll be frozen in a flash," Mrs. Saks said. "Now, where are we meeting them?"

"We turn right at the light and watch for the Valley Diner. I heard last summer that local clowns call it the VD. Just remind me not to trust the cooking."

They pulled into a parking space in front of the diner, climbed out of the car and went in, where they spotted two men in a booth. They were wearing matching heavy flannel jackets and each needed a shave.

"Mrs Saks?" the taller man said. "I'm Captain Spot, and this here is Lester, my first mate."

"We're kind of a team," Lester said. "Other fishers call us the 'Spot-Less' crew." He giggled in a high-pitched tone, then looked at Spot.

Mrs. Saks noticed Lester was missing a few teeth as he smiled.

"Come join us," said the captain. He partially stood in the booth and nodded at the empty bench. The ladies made their way to the booth and sat across from the sailors.

"We already ordered," he said. "The omelettes are pretty good, if you're hungry. Lester here favours the poutine."

"They use real cheese curds here," Lester said. "Some good!"

"We had breakfast earlier," Emma said. "We're here about chartering your boat. We want to see if we can locate any of those sharks on the news."

"I know about where they been seen," Spot said. "But I'm having a little engine work done tomorrow. We could take you out the following afternoon."

"How much would it cost for a couple of hours?" Mrs. Saks said.

"I'll have to check the latest cost of fuel," Spot said. "I'll give you a call tomorrow, and you can decide then. We can pick you up at the dock in Port Medway if it's a go. But we'll need to be paid up front in cash."

"That's fine," Mrs. Saks said. "We're staying up at Stillwaters Centre, and I can cash a check at the desk there. They keep a bunch on hand for change."

"Wouldn't it be nice to have enough money to keep a bunch on hand?" Spot shook his head, and Lester smiled.

"Thank you," Mrs Saks said. "Good luck with your engine work, and I'll talk to you tomorrow." She peered at Lester, who was still grinning. He was, she thought, a very unattractive sailor.

She and Emma got to their feet, smiled, and left the diner.

"What do you think?" Emma said when they were in the car.

"They seem legitimate, but I'll ask Moses at Stillwaters about them. He knows everything that goes on around here."

"Maybe we should have asked him this morning,."

"He wasn't around," Mrs. Saks said. "He's helping out Nipper with a delivery at the liquor store while the men are on Cape Breton. But we'll see him tomorrow and get the scoop. He might show up for pizza tonight, but my guess is he'll go straight home from the Nipper's. That reminds me. I want to drop by there sometime and pick up a bottle of wine."

"What now?" Emma said, fastening her seat belt.

"Now we go back and have a hot cup of tea," Mrs. Saks said. "And then, if we feel up to it, we can take a stroll on the beach. The sun feels warm for this time of year. We can scope out the water while we're at it."

She started the Buick and headed out of the diner parking lot.

6: Bad news for dinner

"Welcome, boys," Hagan said as they settled at a table in the otherwise-empty pub. "The menu is a little limited, but what's available is mighty tasty. It's just us three tonight. Lucille dropped me and headed back to see her sister over in Pugwash. Poor girl has a case of the shingles."

Nodding and Toby looked over the offerings and found several fine choices. Toby ordered fish and chips, while Nodding opted for beef short rib on mashed potatoes. Hagan chose a large bowl of seafood chowder. All three were happy with water to drink.

"Can I ask why we're here?" Toby said. "I appreciate the royal treatment, but it's a bit out of the way this time of year."

"Fair question," Hagan said. "Tomorrow I want to show you fellers a bit of land I bought just across the road. Then, if it's okay, the following day I'd like to catch a ride back to Port Medway with you. Lucille will head home from Pugwash.""

"No problem," Nodding said. "There's plenty of room in the Subaru. Should make an enjoyable road trip."

They paused as their meals arrived.

"Looks mighty tasty," Toby said. He spread tartar sauce on the fried fish. "Are you planning to build something on the land?"

"Truth be told, I bought the land to be buried in. Boys, I found out last week I have cancer, so I'm doing some planning."

"Lordy," Toby said. "Where is it?" He reached over and softly squeezed Hagan's wrist.

"My pancreas," Hagan said. "Too late to fight it. Doctor gives me one, maybe two months."

Nodding stared at Hagan, who looked back and smiled. "It's okay, Dave. I'm fine with it. Really. So here's my plan. We enjoy dinner tonight. Tomorrow morning we go over and I'll show you the land. Then after lunch we need to spend some time on business matters before we finish with a lobster dinner. The next day we head for home. That sound okay?"

"Are you scared?" Nodding said.

"I ain't happy," Hagan said. "But I'm not scared. Nothing I can do about it, you know? At least I have time to get things taken care of before it gets bad. I gotta look at it that way."

"How are you feeling right now?" Toby said.

"I got some pain pills for when it starts to get serious," Hagan said. "Solid foods don't work good, so I'm living on soups. Like tomorrow's lobster for me will be blended into a soup. Liquids stay down good so far."

"So there's nothing you can do?" Toby said.

"I could try chemo or radiation to delay it, but that means lying in bed a few weeks more until it kills me. That ain't no way to go. Lucille and I talked it all out. Now, enjoy your dinners. No more depressing talk."

They avoided any further talk of cancer, but the rest of the meal was quiet. They opted to skip dessert, so after dinner they went up to their rooms. They agreed to meet for breakfast before they visited the land Hagan had purchased.

Nodding glanced at the television as he entered his room but left it off. Instead, he called Kenzie.

"I know," she said. "Lucille called before supper and told us."

"I guess I'll find out more tomorrow," Nodding said. "It's such a shock. Hagan seemed so healthy just a couple of weeks ago. He doesn't look sick now, just a little thin."

"There's nothing any of us can do," she said. "We'll have to wait and see how things develop. Just go to bed and get a good night's sleep. Tomorrow might be a hard day for you. For all of us,"

"I wish you were here."

"Me too, but it's only a couple of days. Call me tomorrow when you have a chance. I'll be here all day."

They hung up, and Nodding crawled into the fresh sheets and fell asleep.

7: Boats Aren't Cheap

Captain Spot called just before lunch. Mrs. Saks and Emma were upstairs in the apartment. Mrs. Saks was drinking a cup of tea, while Emma was reading headlines on her cell phone.

"Repairs are going well and I got the latest cost of fuel," he said. "Total will come to four hundred eighty dollars for three hours. I don't know if that's too much or if you still want to go out tomorrow."

"My goodness," Mrs. Saks said. "It's a bit dear, but we'll go through with it."

"Sounds good," Spot said. "I'll pick you up at one o'clock and drive you over to the Medway dock, and Lester will be there. Can you have the cash by then?"

"I'll have it ready when you get here," Mrs. Saks said. "Thank you." She shook her head and frowned at the mobile. This was not going well!

She hung up and looked up at Emma. "He says it'll cost almost five hundred dollars."

"Sounds a bit expensive to me. But I'll still split the cost, Anne Marie."

"I admit I feel a little suspicious," Mrs. Saks said. "Something seems a little bit off, but I can't put my finger on it. Maybe I should drive down and take a good look at that boat?"

"They might see your car," Emma said. "It's above freezing out there, so you sit tight here, and I'll take the Harley for a spin. Even if they see me, I'll be wearing my leathers and my helmet. Besides, I feel like I need some fresh air."

"Just be careful. There could be icy spots on the back roads."

"I won't take any chances," Emma said.

She already had her leather riding clothes out and was pulling on the pants. She zipped up her jacket and grabbed the bright red helmet. "I won't be long, Anne Marie. I have my phone."

"Be safe, now," Mrs. Saks said. But the door had already closed.

Emma pushed the elevator button and rode it down to the ground floor as a treat for her left knee. It had been a bit stiff recently. She gave a wave to Kenzie, who was sitting behind the main counter, then went out to the parking lot. She took the cover off her Harley, folded it and left it next to the Buick, then climbed into the saddle and fired up the engine. The quiet roar always gave her a thrill, so she smiled as she kicked into gear and glided out of the parking lot.

A little time to herself would be refreshing. These other folks were being supportive, but maybe they weren't as convinced as she was. Tomorrow would demonstrate just how right she was.

Emma kept her speed down as she cruised past the fire department and the turn to Nipper's liquor store. At the intersection she turned left and fired up the engine. She believed this road was always clear this time of year, so she rode the centre line without fear.

She kept her face shield down to stay warm, but smiled as she roared along the road out to the 103. She much preferred these back roads with their curves and hills to the highway. Speeds were higher there, true, but truck traffic always made Emma nervous..

Today she was lucky. Traffic was light, and, in what seemed like a flash, Emma glided into Liverpool. She cruised past the super market and several blocks of houses until she came to the water.

She glanced down from the bridge and saw the boat, then

turned down the access road and made her way alongside the dock. She pulled to a stop when she saw three men she didn't recognize working on the engine compartment. They were wearing heavy green coveralls and matching toques.

She dismounted the cycle and stepped toward the boat.

One of the men saw her and stepped ashore. "Can I help?" he said. "We aren't blocking the water, I hope."

"Not at all," Emma said. She pulled off her helmet. "I was looking for Captain Spot?"

"I don't know any Captain Spot. But I'm from Yarmouth, just here to replace my fuel pump."

"Isn't this his boat?" Emma made sure no other boats were in sight.

"My brother and I own and work this boat. Our name is Green," he said. "Like I said, I don't know this Spot fella, but I really don't know folks here."

"I'm sorry to bother you," Emma said. "Good luck with your repairs." She started to pull her helmet on.

"Thanks," Green said. "We'll probably be here another day or two. This pesky repair is taking longer than we hoped."

He stepped back onto the boat. The other two men were waiting for him, and one of them gave a short wave to Emma.

"Something is rotten here," she said out loud. "I need to get back to the apartment right away quick. Here that old boat isn't even theirs. If I hadn't stopped to chat I would have assumed it was legit."

She fired up her Harley, turned around, and sprayed gravel as she took off. She peered at the boat as she went, noticing the name 'Voyager' on the stern. It made her smile as she roared out.

What could Spot and Lester have in mind? It seemed pretty clear to Emma. They were planning to collect the money from two helpless old women, and worse! Well, those hooligans would be in for a surprise!

Emma turned onto the 103 and opened up the Harley. They had a day to prepare with no time to dilly-dally!

8: The nearby meadow

Breakfast was a continental buffet. Nodding and Toby helped themselves to fruit, decadent pastries and mugs of strong coffee.

"Dang," Toby said after tasting the pastry. "This beats my usual bowl of cereal with sliced banana. But my waist wouldn't like it, so please don't start featuring these goodies at home."

"I won't," Nodding said. "Our guests like pretty standard eggs and toast. But maybe a treat on Christmas."

"Lordy. I wouldn't mind a bit."

They finished breakfast and each headed up to his room to freshen up and get a coat. They met in the parking lot, where they found Hagan waiting. They climbed into the Subaru. Nodding paused at the end of the drive.

"Turn right here," Hagan said. "Watch for a driveway half a kilometre on the left: that's where we're headed."

The driveway was a grassy lane and easy to follow. Before long the lane came into a large meadow. Nodding stopped and they climbed out.

"This was clear cut years ago," Hagan said. "When it grew back, the owner missed this meadow, so he had it trimmed back."

"It's a beautiful spot," Toby said. "That one large pine near the edge of the clearing just stands out."

"I agree," Hagan said. "I always feel right peaceful here. I bought it years ago, thinking I might build a cabin someday. Well, life changes your plans."

"It must be hard knowing you can't retire here after all," Nodding said.

"Lucille said it was too rustic for camping, and she much prefers the guest rooms up at the distillery. But this place was almost magical, and I kept thinking about it. It's like I belong here. So I've set up with that monument feller near Sydney. When I pass, Preacher, I'd ask you to spread my ashes here under the big pine. The monument guy will put a little stone near the tree. That's what Lucille wants. Then the distillery gets the land to use as a park or hiking area with the understanding no new building will take place. I'll rest easy. Just me here in the pines, with the rippling creek flowing through."

"And Dave," Hagan added, "if you can help Lucille plan some kind of farewell lunch and then set it up with the distillery folks, it would make things a lot easier for her."

"Of course," Nodding said.

"Thank you both," Hagan said. "Now let's go get some warm lunch. Ain't no real snow yet, but it's frosty out here."

Nodding took a last look around the clearing as they hiked back to his car. They climbed in as he started the engine and turned up the heat, then drove back to the distillery. The spreading warmth felt good. The sun was bright in Hagan's clearing, but the air was frosty.

Soup and sandwiches were waiting for them in the pub. Hagan stopped at the desk, then joined them at the table. He chose his blended seafood chowder, while Nodding and Toby opted for bowls of chili. A plate of chicken salad sandwiches looked tempting as well.

"Got a problem back home," Hagan said, sitting down. "Phone message from Jean. Said the old ladies think they'll be robbed tomorrow afternoon by the guys who own the boat they were renting. Moses is still helping Nipper, but he'll be at the lodge tomorrow. Jean sounded nervous."

"We won't be back until dinner time," Toby said.

"What if we leave after we eat?" Nodding said. "We could get back around midnight."

"Got an idea," Hagan said. "We could leave after lunch and spend the night in Truro. Then we'd be home in time and not be all worn out."

"We could have our business meeting on the road," Nodding

said. "Used to be a nice motel in Truro called The Paradise Lodge, but I think it closed."

"It was closed for a few months," Hagan said. "But it got bought and it's open again. We could spend the night there."

"Sounds like a plan," Toby said. "I can call and make a reservation before we leave."

"Put the reservation in my name for three rooms," Hagan said. "Then we'll get their bigger rooms."

"Do they know you?" said Nodding.

"I hope so," Hagan said. "I bought the place in August because Lucille liked the indoor swimming pool. Has one of them sliding boards and a hot tub. Anyhow, it's almost always full up. Still haven't figured out why it closed last winter."

"I'll call right after lunch," Toby said. "By then this chili will have warmed me right up. I definitely felt a nip in the air this morning."

After a quick lunch they went to their rooms, got their coats and suitcases, and met at the office for an early check-out.

"Paradise is ready for us," Toby said. "I called Jean, too. Told her we'd changed plans and would be home tomorrow about noon."

"Then let's roll," Nodding said.

He looked around the pub and dining room and decided to bring Kenzie in warmer weather. Autumn would be scenic, too, with bright maples next to green pines.

They stowed their luggage and coats in the Subaru, climbed in, and drove out of the distillery lot towards the causeway to mainland Nova Scotia. The drive along the coast would provide colourful scenery for their business meeting.

Hagan had a briefcase with him in the back seat, and opened it once they passed through Mabou. "I went through all this with my lawyer last week, so once you fellas agree, it'll be made final. When I go under, he'll get in touch with you. I hope we can agree with the plan today. That way none of us has to worry."

"Whatever you want, we'll agree," Toby said.

"Toby's right," Nodding said. "You've been great to work with this past year. We'll do our best to make things easier for you."

"Let's get at it, then," Hagan said. "I have the plans here, so if you two agree, I'll have copies sent to you next week."

He pulled out a legal pad with notes for reference. "Everything depends on keeping Stillwaters open for another summer. If it closes before then, everything we outline today is over. My mother's will made that very clear."

"Dave and I have agreed about that," Toby said. "We both want it to stay open for years. Moses and Virginia agree to stay on, too."

"I'm thankful you feel that way," Hagan said. "You fellas are great, more than I probably deserve. I hope you'll still be on board after today."

"Fire away," Toby said.

"Okay. This past year Lucille has been great, but she has no interest in Port Medway or Stillwaters. So I've decided to split you all and Lucille apart. She has some charities and such she wants to support up in the city, so you'll be on your own down on the South Shore."

"Will we work through your lawyer?" Nodding said.

"No. That's the big change. When I'm gone, there will be new owners of the centre. They will make the decisions, as long as you stay open through next year."

"I'm afraid to ask," Toby said. "Who are the new bosses?"

"You are," Hagan said. "You two and Virginia each will own a third of the retreat. Moses will inherit my half of the liquor store, but I hope he'll still work with you guys. He knows every squeaky hinge on the property and what needs to be fixed, but he doesn't want to be a boss."

"Lordy," Toby said. "Dave and I did our best last summer, but we had to learn as we went. I hate to say it, but I don't know if we're good enough to be in charge. This ain't exactly a field where where we have experience."

"Listen up, boys," Hagan said. "I saw the books this fall. My mother was losing money each year. The lottery win saved her from having to close up. You guys brought in a modest profit. You are damn good enough to own the place. We can't compete with the big resorts nearby. But you know what your customers said would bring them back? They loved the food and warmth of the retreat. They mentioned the clean rooms and main building. And they all praised the chapel services and workshops. That's how you guys made last summer a success. And one more detail the guests mentioned was the kids of staff and guests having fun. It made coming to Stillwaters a family affair. All of that is your doing, and I thank you for it."

"Hagan, Toby and I needed a change in our lives, and you offered us a new path," Nodding said. "I will always be grateful for that, and this new change is almost too kind to comprehend."

"Take a few days to think about it," Hagan said. "I still have to talk with Virginia and Moses. I talked it over with Nipper and he's happy to work with Moses, but he's been thinking about retiring soon. You're pretty quiet, Preacher. What's up?"

"I've been thanking Jesus for giving me a new path in life. And for putting you in my life, Hagan. Thank you. I guess we should keep this quiet until you talk with Moses and Virginia?"

"Give me two days," Hagan said. "My attorney will deliver a copy of my will to each of you when it's okay to discuss it. That way I can answer any questions while I'm still around,"

"Fair enough," Nodding said. "We'll be at the causeway in a few minutes. I'll stop just after that to fill the tank, if anyone wants to visit the washroom."

Following the fuel stop, the drive to Truro was quiet. Hagan slept in the back seat until Nodding pulled into the Paradise parking lot. The lot was full of cars, so Nodding was happy they had reservations.

Toby grabbed Hagan's suitcase with his own and they stepped into the lobby.

9: Return to Paradise

"Welcome to Paradise, It's good to see you, Mr. Hagan." A young man behind the counter smiled at them. "We have three of our executive rooms reserved for you."

"Great. Thanks," Hagan said.

"I tried to book the suite Mrs. Hagan prefers, but it's closed after the accident." He looked down at the counter, blushing. He glanced up, then swung to look at the office doorway.

"What accident?," Hagan said. "No one mentioned an accident."

"It's all my fault," a woman said, and the young lady Nodding had met on his last stay stepped out of the office and to the counter. "We had a request for the suite after you and your wife were here last week. It was from a movie company, and they wanted the suite for their big star."

"Someone famous?" Toby said.

"That's where I screwed up," the young woman said. "I tried to stay cool and took the credit card information for the next night. It was in the film company's name, so I never got the guest's name. It was reserved for "Big Adventures Film Group.""

"Did the credit card accept the charge?" Hagan said.

"No problem there," the young man said. "The next day three guys came with a camera and lights to set up. So it wasn't for the star to stay, but to film in the room."

"Did you meet the star? Who was it?" Toby said.

"That was how the problem started," the young lady said. "We never saw either of the actors. They must have come in a side door. We could have prevented the accident if they came in the front door."

"So what happened?" Hagan said. He watched as the young man and woman looked at each other.

"They were here to make an adult film," the young lady said. "No one ever told us they were filming here, let alone making an adult film."

"Mistakes happen," Hagan said. "But what happened? What was the accident?"

Something wasn't being explained. He glanced at Toby, who shrugged.

The young woman looked down, blushing.

"Big adventures refers to the actors," the young man said. "The two that were here each weighed more than three hundred pounds."

"Lordy," Toby said.

"We don't know exactly how, but they broke the bed frame and a chair," the young woman said. "We charged the credit card, but the new furniture isn't here yet."

"Now that's some story," Hagan said. "You folks handled it right, so I got no complaints. I bet you never expected that to happen in Paradise."

"No sir," the young woman said. "But we won't let them come back."

"I got nothing against folks having fun or even making movies," Hagan said. "But next time they can find another motel to visit."

"Sounds good to me," Toby said. "We'll have to keep our eyes open at Stillwaters for movie makers."

"Probably not an issue," Nodding said. "We don't have fancy suites, and our rooms all have twin beds and Bibles."

"Then we can relax," Hagan said. "Let's drop our suitcases and go next door to Jimmy's. I could use some hot soup. And no mention of this to Lucille or she won't come back."

Jimmy's was part of a chain, but it had offerings each of them liked. Hagan ordered fresh tomato soup, while Toby opted for a double cheese burger and poutine. Nodding enjoyed a chicken Caesar salad after a shared nachos appetizer.

They agreed to have the Paradise continental breakfast at seven-thirty the next day, so they could be on the road by eight. They should be able to be home before any problems developed. Toby was still concerned, since Mrs. Saks was involved.

It had been a tiring day, and Nodding went straight to bed after dinner.

10: Nipper's Fantasy

Emma parked her trike and hurried inside without putting the cover on. She waved at Kenzie at the desk, then rode the elevator up to Anne Marie's apartment.

"It's a setup," she said, getting out of her leathers. "They don't own the boat. So when they show up tomorrow, they plan to rob us. They outright lied to us, Anne Marie."

"I'll run over to the liquor store and tell Moses and Nipper. I hope David and Toby get back in time. I'll ask Jean or Kenzie to call the distillery and fill them in. If they dilly-dally they might miss everything. We'd be in one big pickle then."

Mrs. Saks got her coat out of the closet and put it on.

"I'll give a couple of girls I ride with a call, just in case," Emma said. "I'm one of the few who puts her cycle away for the winter."

"What can any of them do?"

"In case they get our money, a Harley can follow them and fill in the Mounties. I don't think we could keep up in your Buick. Besides, the helmets all have microphones, don't you know."

"Let's hope it doesn't come to that!"

They rode down in the elevator to the first floor and Mrs Saks went out to start the Buick. Emma paused at the desk to fill in Kenzie, then hurried out and climbed into the car.

She turned to face Mrs. Saks. "I hope this helps. I trust your friend Moses completely, but i don't have much confidence in that Nipper, from what I've heard."

Mrs. Saks took off, pulling into the Hagan's Haven parking lot within minutes. A pickup truck belonging to Moses was the only car in the lot, parked next to the golf cart Nipper used to move beer from the storage shed to the loading dock.

"I'll make my call and spread the word," Emma said, pulling out her mobile. "I'll be right in."

She peered at her phone to find the number as Mrs. Saks hurried into the store. No one picked up on her first call, but she connected on her second call.

Moses was reading an invoice and looked up as she came in. "Mrs. Saks," he said. "What's wrong?"

"That Captain Spot doesn't own a boat," she said. "They're coming to steal our money just after lunch tomorrow. I think we should call the Mounties right away quick."

"It might be a misunderstanding," Moses said. "Before we involve the RCMP, let's be sure. I'll be there to meet them, and Toby and David are planning to be home by then with Chet. Three of us can handle whatever happens."

He looked up as Emma came into the store. "You must be Ms. Mitchell. We're planning our strategy for tomorrow."

"I just talked to one of the girls in my motorcycle club," Emma said. "A few of them will show up here, just in case. If those scalawags try to escape, they'll follow them and report their whereabouts. A couple have been customers here, so they'll meet in your parking lot."

"This is getting more interesting by the minute," said an older, pink-faced man limping towards them from the wine section of the store. "So nice to see you again, Mrs. Saks," he said, raising his cane. "Floyd Eisenhower, Ms. Mitchell. But please call me Nipper."

"And I'm Emma. That's a beautiful cane you have there."

"Thank you. Mercy. I bought it because it's a copy of the cane Bat Masterson carried in the American West."

"It's quite ornate," Mrs. Saks said.

"But perhaps not historically accurate," Nipper said. "Since I stopped devouring candy and got my sugars under control, I've been doing some research into Masterson and Wyatt Earp in their old age. And I've discovered there are no photographs whatsoever of Bat Masterson with a cane. None."

"I saw a western movie about him once," Emma said. "He was a spiffy dresser. He wore a derby hat, even on those dusty streets."

"I'm not a derby fan," Nipper said. "So I ordered a hat like John Wayne used to wear in his movies, a genuine Stetson. It cost a pretty penny and my ears still get cold on days like this. Mercy."

"That's because we aren't in Arizona," Moses said. "We're in Nova Scotia, so we keep our ears warm by wearing toques."

"I know," Nipper said. "But I do admire the cowboy hats. I even ordered a plastic roof shaped like a Stetson for my golf cart."

"You and that cart," Moses said. "I remember when you first got it, you gave it a name."

"Bucephalus," Nipper said. "War horse of Alexander the Great."

"Goodness," Emma said. "I would have guessed the Batmobile, since you liked the cowboy with a cane."

"Now that's a thought," Nipper said. "I just might change its name, since I've been researching those fellows. But I confess I scoot around with it more often when the weather warms up. It's a bit brisk these days."

"Speaking of staying warm," Mrs Saks said, "I want to buy a bottle of wine for Christmas Eve. Do you have any from the Spatola Italian Vineyards?"

"I don't recall," Nipper said. "But I'll check and get some in for Christmas. I normally carry only what our customers request. I'm no expert on wine, I admit. I get visits from vineyards in the Valley, but I honestly don't know what I should keep in stock. It's all I can do to keep up with the craft beers these days."

"Listen here," Mrs. Saks said. "When spring springs, you can close up for a day. I'll drive you and Moses over to the Valley, and we'll visit a couple of wineries. I know of two that serve a tasty lunch, so the trip will be an adventure."

"I'll treat for lunch," Nipper said. "What about it, Moses? Sounds like fun. Having a tasty lunch out on the patio on a sunny spring day."

"Tell you what," Moses said. "I'll stay and keep the store open. I'm not a wine drinker."

"First things first," Emma said. "We have to get through tomorrow. Those hooligans are coming to steal our money."

"We'll be ready," Moses said.

"That's what Thomas Hardy would say in his books," Mrs Saks said. "But then he'd say 'if no misfortune happens.'"

"And I bet it did," Emma said. "But we're as ready as possible. So let's keep our fingers crossed."

11: Misfortune happens

Nodding pulled the Subaru up to the front door after breakfast. Toby loaded their bags while Hagan settled in the back seat, and then left Truro on the 102. Toby glanced back after ten minutes and saw Hagan was asleep. He nudged Nodding and let him know, so they stayed quiet until they turned onto the 103,

Traffic was light until they swung past the Halifax airport and turned towards home. Then the flow slowed, until they came to a full stop shortly after Hammonds Plains.

"It wasn't this bad on our way up," Toby said. "They're twinning a whole stretch of the 103. But at least we've been moving."

"We should still be back on time," Nodding said. "But maybe give Moses a call so he can be there early."

"Good idea," Toby said. He punched a number into his mobile and brought Moses up to date. He and Nipper were in the store, just waiting for word from the ladies.

"Okay, good," he said, hanging up. He swung around to include Hagan. "Moses will go over soon, just to be ready. And we're moving again. Great!"

~

"It's the battery," Moses said, coming into the store. "I gotta call Toby. What a time for it to fail."

"We better get over there," Nipper said. "You lock up while I fire up Bucephalus. Not likely to get any customers anyway."

He grabbed his cowboy hat and cane and hobbled out the door. He climbed into the cart, started the motor, put the cart in gear and held the brake pedal down for Moses, who was locking the store.

As Moses ran out and climbed onto the seat beside him, six large motorcycles wheeled into the parking area. The riders all wore black leather jackets and red helmets. Most of their faces were hidden by their helmet shields, but Moses saw that two of the riders had long white braids. One of them seemed to be in charge.

The leader pulled up next to Nipper. "They need us now," she called, then pulled back to the other riders. They roared their engines, and Moses gripped his seat firmly.

"Let's roll," Nipper said.

He stomped on the gas and the cart lurched forward, spitting loose gravel as it swung out of the parking lot and onto the road.

Behind him there was a roar as the six motorcycles fell in after the cart.

~

"Almost there," Nodding said as they drove into Port Medway. He slowed as they approached the intersection.

"Lordy," Toby said. "Looky there."

Hagan sat up and looked out as they slowed for the intersection. "Go Nipper," he called, gripping the back of Nodding's seat.

At the intersection, Nipper turned his golf cart in front of them. Moses was sitting beside him and holding on as the cart slid into the turn. Behind it were six motorcycles, following in formation.

"Now who are those guys?" Toby said. "Dang!"

Nodding turned behind the motorcycles, following closely. They raced up the road towards the Stillwaters parking lot.

Hagan leaned over, watching as they passed the fire station.

"Two Mounties following," he said, as the police car turned onto the road behind them. The cruiser's siren shrieked, almost drowning the roar of the motorcycles.

Ahead of them, Nipper swung into the lot. Mrs. Saks was standing with Emma near a white pickup truck. Lester was in front of the truck and turned to see the golf cart drive into the lot.

Nipper hit the brakes, but the cart slid and smacked Lester enough to push him against the pickup's bumper.

"Got him!" Nipper said, putting the cart in park.

Lester looked wildly about. He pushed off to run, but the motorcycles formed a line to block any escape.

The police car pulled in behind the golf cart.

"The other one is inside robbing the desk," Emma said, pointing at the door.

"I would have shot him, but my gun is missing," Mrs. Saks said.

"You wait right here," one of the Mounties called. They both sprinted to the door and cautiously opened it before going in.

"It isn't even your boat," said Emma. "The nerve of you men."

"We wouldn't be taking a boat out in weather like this," Lester said. "Them lobstermen are crazy."

"But they make an honest living," Nipper said.

"I hope the Mounties got your partner," Mrs. Saks said, peering at the door to the lodge.

Just then the door opened and the Mounties came out with Captain Spot in handcuffs. They helped him into the rear seat of their car, then walked over and put handcuffs on Lester.

"What were you thinking, Lester?" one of the Mounties asked. "You've only been out of jail for a month."

"You picked the wrong folks to rob," the other Mountie said. "Those women stopped you in your tracks."

"He only got that far because I didn't have my gun," Mrs. Saks said, glaring at the patrol car.

"Mercy," Nipper said. "This isn't the wild west."

"Mr. Eisenhower is right," the Mountie said, cuffing Lester. "If you had a gun, we'd be cuffing you, too."

"We need to get statements from the ladies," the other Mountie said. "The rest of you can get in out of the cold."

The motorcycle riders parked their bikes and followed the men into the warmth of the lobby. Kenzie and Virginia were behind the front desk, smiling.

"Are you gals okay?" Toby said.

"Thanks to Kenzie, we're fine," Virginia said. "That man never had a chance."

"What happened?" Nodding said.

"They showed up early, so Mrs. Saks and Emma went out to meet them," Kenzie said. "But the boss man came straight in and demanded the money box. He was scary, so I handed it over, but just then we heard the motorcycles and siren as you all got here. So he took the money box and ran into the elevator to escape."

"How'd you stop him?" Toby said. "He must not have gone far."

"I just hit the elevator emergency switch under the counter," Kenzie said. "It cuts power to the elevator, so he was trapped in the dark until the police came in. Then I brought the elevator back to the lobby and they arrested him."

"You're the hero of the day," Virginia said. "I was too scared to move."

She smiled at Kenzie, who blushed.

"Well, I thought they might try to rob us as well as the ladies," Kenzie said. "So there were only twelve dollars and some of Wyatt's play dollars in the box. The rest of the cash is hidden away. It's actually in Wyatt's toy box,"

"Great thinking," Hagan said. "They didn't have a chance."

"A happy ending for the good guys," Nipper said. "But I better get back to the store, folks."

"I'll stay here and ride home with Virginia," Moses said. "I'll get the truck towed tomorrow for a new battery."

"We need to get on the road, too," one of the motorcycle riders said. "A couple of us aren't great at driving after dark."

Toby looked at Nodding and raised his eyebrows.

"It gets dark early," Nodding said. "And we have an empty motel next door. Why not let us turn up the heat and give you a night to rest up? I can cook up a warm dinner, too."

"It's the least we can do," Toby said. "And I'll vouch for Dave's cooking. It's worth staying just to enjoy dinner."

"Then we'll take you up on your offer," one of the women said, stepping forward. "I'm Anke Hausmann, president of the Grey Ghost Riders. My sister, Abby Whynot, and I started the club after we lost our husbands."

"We didn't want to spend the rest of our lives playing Mah Jong indoors," Abby said. "Tea parties aren't for us."

"Just the opposite," Anke said. "I haven't told Emma or the girls yet, but we got news there have been some Bigfoot sightings up near Ecum Secum. We'll have to take a ride to check it out. Think if we actually see it. What a hoot!"

"That'll be a chilly trip," Kenzie said.

"Oh, we're not that crazy," Abby said. "We'll wait until spring to ride that far."

"Besides," Anke said, "we have to be here to spend Christmas with our grandchildren. Christmas is for families, you know."

The other women agreed, and Virginia led them to their rooms while Moses went to crank up the heat.

"I better get started on dinner," Nodding said. "How about spaghetti or a tuna salad plate? Our options are a bit limited until the holiday orders arrive next week."

"Either one sounds delicious," Kenzie said. "I'll come up and help. Either entree is pretty simple to prepare."

"I might try some of both," Toby said. "But first I'll take Hagan home, unless you want to stay for supper."

"I appreciate the offer," Hagan said. "But today has been enough excitement for me. Thanks, Toby."

Moses got the heat going in the motel rooms, then opened the storage barn for the ladies to park their cycles. Wyatt's school bus dropped him in time for him to follow Emma's cycle as she rode it to the barn.

"Think you'd like to own one someday?" Anke said, seeing his excitement. She dismounted her cycle as he watched her carefully. He stepped forward and touched the headlight, then stepped back.

"Maybe one a little smaller," he said. "These are pretty big."

"Tell you what," Anke said. "I'll call your mom this summer and set a time to come by and give you a ride. I have a grandson about your age, and he goes on rides with me when the weather is warm. By the way, your mother stopped a robber and saved the day. So be good to her this evening."

"Cool," Wyatt said. "Thanks." His mom was a hero today!

He watched Anke wheel her Harley into the barn before running to the lodge to find his mother.

12: Everyone knows

For dinner, Nodding shifted furniture so the adults sat around a large table, while the children had their own table in the private room. He prepared chicken tenders and fries for them as a treat, while the adults chose spaghetti with sausage and peppers. Nodding topped off the pasta with mozzarella, then baked it until the cheese melted, as a finishing touch.

"Thank you all for your help and this grand dinner," Emma said. "I suppose our investigation is a failure."

"Exactly what was your investigation?" Anke said. "I never did hear what this was all about."

"Moon men and sharks in cold water," Emma said.

She went on to explain the winter shark reports. "So it must be something secretive, like space beings in disguise. Sharks don't swim in ice water." She took a sip of her tea.

"But it's not icy," Abby said. "My daughter Cairn lives in Liverpool and she read about the sharks online. See, towns like Liverpool have waste water treatment plants. Once the sewage is treated, it flows out in pipes to the ocean. And that warms the salt water around it, making it friendly for them sharks. That's why they stay close to the shore."

"Now I feel like a fool," Mrs. Saks said. "I should have done some research into shark habits."

"Don't be so hard on yourself," Toby said. "None of us thought to learn about waste water. No damage was done, two nasty men were caught, and it's dang near Christmas."

"Thank you," Emma said. "And another thank you for your hospitality. You have been very welcoming to a nosy old lady."

She paused while the motorcycle ladies clapped. They were all grateful for a warm meal and a comfortable bed for the night.

"We'll get out of your hair and head home tomorrow morning."

"Well, I haven't talked to anyone but Kenzie about this," Mrs. Saks said, "but she suggested I stay for Christmas. I don't have any family and Lunenburg can be lonely when you live by yourself."

"Oh, do stay," Nodding said. "We'll make it a festive holiday."

"We have some centre guests coming, too, mostly older single folks," Toby said. "It should be an inspiring time with musical services both Christmas Eve and Christmas morning. "

"Really?" Abby said. "My daughter and her family aren't church goers. So I might just ride over."

"Eight for the evening service and ten on Christmas morning and you're welcome to bring your family," Toby said.

"On Christmas Day we'll have a traditional turkey dinner with all the trimmings," Nodding said. "Toby has already requested butter tarts as part of dinner."

"Oh yeah," Toby said. "I can't get enough of those tasty nibbles."

Kenzie and Toby stayed to help with the dishes, which made loading the large dishwasher a smooth operation.

"I'm going to disappear tomorrow for a visit with my parents up in the city," Nodding said. "Virginia will take care of any deliveries. This will be my first Christmas away from home, so a quick visit will have to do. I'll spend some time with them next month, when we're closed for a spell."

"You can stay another day or two," Toby said. "We're in good shape for the first guests."

"I know," Nodding said. "But my life is here now. I want to come back and celebrate the season with all of you. This is the first

Christmas I'm looking forward to since I was a kid,"

He looked at Kenzie and saw her smile at him. "I realized I don't have any idea about what to give Wyatt for Christmas."

"Well, he's wanted a radio controlled boat," Kenzie said. "But I think he realizes the ocean would be too rough for one. I've got him some clothes and a book, but nothing he can have fun with."

"I'm picking up my old electric train from my parents," Nodding said. "I thought we could set it up in the lobby. I can ask Wyatt to be the chief engineer."

"Oh, he'll love that."

"That gives me an idea," Nodding said. "How would he like a working drone? They make them for kids his age."

"You don't have to get Wyatt anything that fancy, David," she said. "He'll be thrilled just helping with the train set."

"I'm being selfish. I've wanted to see how drones work. Wyatt can show me."

"You're being too generous," Kenzie said. "But thank you."

13: Home and back

The next morning, Nodding grabbed some coffee, left the pot for later risers, and headed for the city. As he swung past Hagan's Haven, he saw Nipper fastening a large plastic cowboy hat to the roof of his golf cart. He honked and smiled as Nipper waved.

He decided to take advantage of the winter freedom to spend more time with Nipper. They both loved Westerns, so there would be plenty to talk about.

This really was his home now, he realized. And these friends were now his family. He hoped he could spend his future with them, where he was happy.

Out on the 103, he smiled again. On his right was the country pub Toby liked for lunch. He'd have to bring Kenzie out to try it. Toby claimed the poutine was the best he'd ever had, with hearty beef gravy and real cheese curds. Once you were in the tourist areas like Mahone Bay, Lunenburg, or even Chester, they dolled up poutine with bits of lobster, chicken gravy, and mozzarella instead of curds. Toby swore by the real deal, so Nodding knew it would be worth trying in this pub.

As he passed the parking lot, he noted more pickup trucks than cars. It was where the locals went for breakfast. He was tempted to turn around and have breakfast, but shook his head and sped up.

Today was for family and doing some Christmas shopping. His first stop was a toy and hobby shop on Spring Garden Road in Hali-fax. They offered five different levels of drones, so he picked out a beginner's model for Wyatt. Then he headed for his parents' house and a day at home. His parents had both retired, so they would be home and expecting him.

He parked in the driveway and walked in through the back door, where the aroma of a roast in the oven enveloped him. Dinner would be festive.

"Anyone home?" he called.

He heard movement from the living room, and someone turned off the television. He realized he had months of news to share as he heard his parents coming toward him.

And in that moment he thought of Kenzie and wished she was with him.

~

After a warm visit and the family dinner, Nodding spent the night in his room, taking time to look over old photos and certificates before climbing into his bed.

The next morning he enjoyed a relaxed breakfast with his parents, before driving back to the South Shore, armed with leftover roast beef in case he got hungry driving. Traffic was light, so he pulled into Stillwaters well before dinner.

He decided to drop the roast beef in the kitchen before going up to his apartment. He took the steps two at a time, happy to be back, then went into the kitchen. He reached for the light switch, then jumped when the light came on, revealing Toby sitting at the table, his face wet with tears.

"Is it Hagan?" Nodding said. "Has he—?"

"Oh no," Toby said, rubbing the tears away. "He's hanging on. He's even planning to come by on Christmas for a bit. It's the opposite, Davy. I've been thanking the good Lord for today, and these tears just started pouring out."

"Why today?" Nodding said, leaving the roast beef on the counter and sitting down across from Toby.

"The letter," Toby said. "I was in the chapel helping Virginia with the decorations when Jean brought it down. I carried it up here so I could read it alone."

He pointed to Nodding's invoice folder. "It's the will, Davy. I put your copy in the folder."

Nodding brought the envelope back to the table.

"The Lord blessed me already with what Hagan did for us," Toby said. "But this is a miracle. I'm a trucker, David, but here I get to spend my days serving God. And now this. Sweet Jesus." He shook his head, and blinked at fresh tears.

"What does it say?" Nodding said, holding his sealed envelope.

"It changes our lives," Toby said. "More than you can imagine."

He wiped his eyes and lowered his voice. "Hagan is leaving each of us a million dollars as well as Stillwaters. It means my daughters can go to university if they want. I never even hoped for that."

Nodding tore open the envelope and scanned the document.

"Besides us, he's leaving a million for Moses and Virginia, and a healthy chunk for Nipper. He's leaving a donation for the fire department and Lucille will inherit the rest." Toby took a deep breath. "We just have to keep Stillwaters open til next fall."

"We already decided we wanted to stay open," Nodding said.

"And I still do," Toby said. "More than ever."

"What about Jean and Kenzie?"

"Hagan doesn't really know them," Toby said. "The same with Virginia's daughters and kitchen help. He's rewarding us because he knows us and we've helped him."

"Makes sense, but wow," Nodding said. "Can we say anything about this?"

"I plan on telling Jean," Toby said. "You can tell Kenzie and your parents, but otherwise I guess we should keep it to ourselves."

"Good idea." Nodding stood up and moved his roast beef to a shelf in the cooler.

"While you're here, I've got a favour to ask," Toby said.

"Shoot," Nodding sat down again.

"I know we have the outside lights on a timer. But on Christmas Eve, could we leave the blue star on all night? I want us to be easy to find if a traveller needs a place to stay."

"Our inn will always have room," Nodding said. "We can leave a room lit all night, too, if you want."

"No need," Toby said. "It's more of a symbol, I guess. But it's the best night to do it. Way back, when I was knee high to a duck, we lived next to a science teacher at the Catholic high school, named Ken. He used to leave a little light turned on in a window all night. I asked him about it once, since my parents always turned everything off. Well, Ken told me he got the idea from the Pope when he was young. He said the Pope left a light on so anyone could come in and find a friend. I like that notion, and I'll feel good about doing it on Christmas Eve."

'We can keep the star lit every night if you want," Nodding said.

"Oh, just the one night is enough," Toby said. "I don't think many pilgrims will wander through Port Medway at night. But thanks for the offer. How was your visit with your folks?"

"It was good. I'm glad I went."

"Say, Jean was up to Bridgewater today buying lunches for the girls and the chicken takeout place had a special on, so she bought more than we can handle. Kenzie and Wyatt are coming over, so wander over about six and join us?"

"Sounds like fun," Nodding said. "Can I bring anything?"

"Nah," Toby said. "It won't be as good as your cooking, but we'll have fun. Jean got some peppermint ice cream, too, so even my picky daughters will be happy."

He stood up and folded his letter into his jacket pocket. "Golly, it's almost Christmas. I better check the pine wreaths in the chapel."

He went out through the dining room, leaving Nodding to re-read the letter he was still holding.

14: Nipper drops in

On December 23rd Nodding was in the kitchen, getting ready for the holiday dinner on Christmas Eve, when he heard the elevator. He was surprised when Nipper Eisenhower limped into the dining room wearing a backpack and leaning on his Bat Masterson cane.

"Merry Christmas, David," Nipper said, putting his backpack on a table. "I'm wearing my festive slippers to get in the spirit. I left Moses in charge and ventured forth to find the Holiday festivities."

He stepped away from the table to let Nodding admire his fluffy green slippers. Each had a blinking red light on the toe. Nodding half expected them to play a carol, but the slippers were quiet.

"I'm just like Rudolf," Nipper said, limping to the table and sitting down. "The lights are fun, but the batteries don't last very long. May I presume you got your letter from Chet's attorney? Moses and I had a chat yesterday about them."

"Yes I did," Nodding said. "It was a real shock."

"The whole deal is a shock. When Chet first let on he was ill, I went home and cried."

"You've been friends for a long time."

"Chet used to work for me until he got his trucking job. Now he owns half the store. He's been good to me, but now I'll be working with Moses."

"How will that be?" Nodding said.

"A big change, but a good one. Moses will be there for support, but he doesn't want to spend all of his days stocking wine shelves.

He wants to keep helping out here."

"That puts more on your plate, Nipper."

"Not really. Moses and I agreed to make some changes. Once we cleared out everything from the States, we liked the smaller inventory. So we kept up the changes. We got rid of the spirits and from now on we'll carry wine and a few craft beers. We're going to offer a variety of cheeses, too. I think the store will have more class as a result."

"That sounds great," Nodding said. "Do either of you know much about wine? I know Moses doesn't drink."

"We're beginners, so we've hired a clerk who will handle the wine. I know cheese and beer. So if Jody doesn't come back for the summer, we can handle it. I'm ready for a change. But I'll certainly miss Jody. Mercy. I do hope she comes back."

"Then I wish you well," said Nodding. "What are you doing for Christmas? You're welcome to join us."

"Thank you, David. I might take you up on Christmas Eve. On Christmas I'm making fondue with Anne Marie since the store will be closed."

"Mrs. Saks?"

"She's our new wine clerk," Nipper said. "We've had several meetings in the past week. She's decided to move to the area. We get along nicely. Chet approves, and darned if he told me he wants to change the name to 'Nipper and Saks Fine Wines'. He says we need to make a fresh start."

"I had no idea," Nodding said.

"Well, she thought of you fellas. Asked me to make a delivery."

Nipper reached into his backpack and pulled out a bottle of French Champagne. "She asked me to drop this off for you. I have another for Jean and Toby. Anne Marie's off meeting with a realtor today about moving here from Lunenburg, or she would have dropped these off herself."

"That was kind of her. Is she planning to rent?"

"She's looking, but there isn't much she likes so far. Most of the houses available are intended for families. They're too big for her to keep up."

Nipper suddenly sat up straight. "I have the solution, by golly. Why didn't I think of it before?"

"Know a good place?" Nodding said.

"Not only that, I own it! When my brother ran the store with me, we bought a duplex house up towards Mill Village. Each side was perfect for one occupant, so we had privacy but could share rides to the store and home. But when Lloyd passed, I cleaned out his side and it's still just sitting there. Haven't really thought about renting it. But she could have it cheaply if I got a ride to work in her Buick. I know Moses and Virginia and Jody would be happy to give up driving me back and forth."

"Sounds like everyone would be a winner," Nodding said.

"I'll give her a call and invite her to see Lloyd's half of the house for starters. But for now, I better get going, David. I didn't plan to keep you from your chores. Is Toby down in his chapel?"

"As far as I know."

"Now there is one devoted man. Say, remember last summer when we chatted about our favourite TV cowboys?"

"You liked *Bonanza*, as I recall."

"I still do," Nipper said. "But since then I've been following Bat Masterson and Wyatt Earp. Both were the real deal, you know. In fact, I've written a yarn about Wyatt Earp's retirement in California, if you'd be interested in reading it some time."

"I'd love to."

"Great," Nipper said, pulling on his backpack. "I'll see you all tomorrow, then. Have fun!"

He tapped his cane on the wooden floor and then was off to the elevator.

15: Time to celebrate!

Twelve Stillwaters guests had made reservations, and eleven showed up on Christmas Eve: four couples and three singles. Nodding served a festive dinner, with seafood as a special entree with haddock and scallops. Kenzie and one of Virginia's daughters served the meal. Nodding had served them earlier, so they wouldn't miss the festive meal. He sprinkled a few chunks of lobster on their plates as a bonus for serving dinner.

After dessert of classic Christmas Crack, Nodding changed from his chef's jacket to a fresh white shirt and tie, then joined Kenzie and Wyatt for a service of Christmas carols in the chapel. Toby led the service, with Jean playing keyboard for the carols.

Their daughters joined Kenzie and Nodding, sitting on either side of Wyatt. They were joined near the rear of the chapel by Abby Whynot and a grandson who knew Wyatt from their hockey team.

Nodding slipped out when the final hymn began and went to the kitchen. He set out a bowl of eggnog and plates of brownies and sugar cookies for the guests. Soon he heard the service ending and glanced out the dining room window. He smiled at the blinking blue star above the gazebo.

"I'm going up to get Wyatt settled."

He turned to see Kenzie in the doorway. "May I take him a cookie?"

"Of course," Nodding said. "The forecast is for some snow tomorrow, so it probably won't be good for flying the drone. I wrapped up the train set, so he'll have something to play with indoors tomorrow. He'll find it in the lobby. I imagine it won't take long until we're hearing train whistles. We might get pretty tired of that whistle. I know my parents did,"

"You're too nice, David. Will I see you later?"

"Mrs. Saks gave me a bottle of champagne. I'll bring it over as soon as things clear out here."

"Good," Kenzie said, wrapping two cookies up in a napkin. "I have a present for you upstairs, so don't be too long."

When the guests had enjoyed their snack and left, Nodding covered the cookies and put the eggnog in the cooler. Then he brought the wrapped train set out of the pantry, turned off the dining room lights, and carried the train set downstairs.

He put the gift near a wall plug, made sure the "for WYATT" label could be seen, then went up to his third-floor apartment. He was excited to see Wyatt's reaction to his presents, but eager to see Kenzie's reaction to his present for her.

On the way to his door he passed the apartment Mrs. Saks used, and heard Christmas music playing. He wondered if she had agreed to look at Nipper's duplex before the fondue.

Just ahead was his door, and across the hall was Kenzie's. Leaning against his door was a large envelope, and for a minute he thought it was the present Kenzie had mentioned. He couldn't imagine what could be in the package.

But when he picked it up, he saw a note on the front:

Merry Christmas, David. Hope you enjoy Wyatt and Bat

– Nipper

"He's been busy," Nodding said, hefting the envelope before putting it down on an end table. He was tempted to look inside, but resisted. Tonight his attention was focused on Kenzie.

He went to his bedroom closet and took out the wrapped drone and another package of batteries. He had planned to give Kenzie her present Christmas morning, but changed his mind when she said she had a gift for him tonight. Besides, he thought, tomorrow he'd be pretty busy. He took down her small package and slid it into his pocket.

He went back to the living room and opened his door. Kenzie's door was opened a bit, the signal that Wyatt was in bed. He left a lamp on, took a deep breath, and smiled.

Nodding stepped across the hallway and slid Wyatt's gift and batteries through the door. Then he went back to his apartment and got the champagne out of his mini-fridge, grabbed two glasses, and went back across the hall, where Kenzie was holding the door open for him.

"How about a Christmas toast?" he said, putting the champagne and glasses on the coffee table.

"That was sweet of Mrs. Saks," she said. "You know I'm not much of a drinker, but this is our first Christmas together, so I'll live it up."

She hugged Nodding, then released him so he could open the wine.

She settled on the couch and watched Nodding pop the champagne cork and pour them each a glass.

"Here's to a Merry Christmas and a happy one for us," he said, raising his glass.

"And a wonderful year ahead," she said, raising her glass to his. Their eyes met and held for a moment.

They each sipped their drinks, then Kenzie pulled a wrapped parcel from beside the couch. "Merry Christmas," she said, handing Nodding the gift.

"It's heavy," Nodding said. He hefted the package and put it in his lap. Kenzie leaned forward to watch him open it.

He tore the paper wrapping and pulled out a heavy wool sweater. "Wow, this is beautiful. Thank you!"

He leaned over and kissed Kenzie, then held the sweater up to admire it.

"It's from Sweden," she said. "I had my uncle Sven send it from Uppsala, where he lives. Their sweaters are better for cold winters than the fleece ones you get around here. And I bet this building will get pretty cold this winter."

"I think you're right. At least the apartments have their own baseboard heaters. But this sweater will keep me toasty. Thank you."

"Can I ask you a question about what happens after the winter? I know you and Toby promised to keep Stillwaters open through next fall, but what about after that? Toby has kids in school and hockey, so he and Jean are growing roots here. But what about David? Now you can afford to go anywhere if you want."

"Toby and I have plans to keep this place open beyond next fall. And we hope everyone will want to stay, too, though people may have other dreams to follow."

"Do you, David?" Kenzie shifted to face him. "Where do you see yourself in five years?"

Nodding felt himself blushing and realized it was time to choose his future. This time it was his to choose and not react to another's plan. And he was ready. He had no doubts or hesitation as he looked at Kenzie.

This was love, he realized. He was in love!

"I do enjoy this old place," he said. "But I don't really care where I'll be in the future. What does matter is that I want to be with you, wherever you are." For once, he had been honest and shared his feelings.

He slipped the small package out of his pocket and offered it to her. "Will you marry me?"

"Oh, David. Are you sure? I come with Wyatt, and my ex said I was a worthless wife."

"I want to be a family with you and Wyatt. Forget your ex. I know you and I love you and I want to live with you, no matter where we decide to be."

"Then yes," Kenzie said, moving into his arms. "I want to be your wife. I want to be a family with you and let Wyatt grow up with you as his father."

She sat back up and held up the small package. "Can I open it?"

"It's my grandmother's ring," Nodding said as she unwrapped it. "My mother gave it to me when I spent the night. We can take it to a jeweller and you can pick out a setting you like and make it yours."

"I love it. I never had a diamond before, David." She slipped the ring onto her finger.

"I saw Nipper yesterday and our conversation gave me an idea. You know how, if you turn left from the driveway, the road winds past houses and ends up by the lighthouse at Medway Head?"

"It's pretty down there. Wyatt and I rode there on our bikes in October. I did think there were lots of mosquitoes."

"I drove out there this morning. There are two houses for sale before the lighthouse, so maybe the three of us should take a look. If we're a family, we can't stay in these apartments all year."

"You're right," Kenzie said. "Gosh. This changes everything, but in a good way. This is the best Christmas I've ever had. I love you, David Nodding."

"And I love you, Kenzie Pearce."

"My married name brings back bad memories. I want to be a Nodding. Kenzie Nodding sounds better to me."

"Then that's what it'll be," Nodding said.

"Do you want to stay over tonight? I know we've always gone

home because of what people would say and all, but now we're engaged."

"I want to, but I won't. Tomorrow morning is Christmas, and Wyatt is going to wake up eager to enjoy his Christmas morning. Let's not confuse him and disrupt his day. We'll have time to explain it all to him later."

"You're already a loving father, David. I want to tell him our news, but you're right. I want his Christmas here to be happy and not confusing."

Nodding filled their glasses and they sat together for a half hour. But the next day would be a busy one, so finally he slipped out and took his new sweater across the hall. The forecast warned of a cold snap by New Year's, so he looked forward to showing off his present.

In his apartment, he hung the sweater on a chair for morning. On the way into his bedroom he grabbed Nipper's manuscript. It was tempting, so he carried it into his bedroom.

He undressed, looked out the window, and smiled to see snowflakes starting to fall. He climbed into bed and read the first few pages of Nipper's book. He liked it and wanted to read more, but it was late.

"I'll be back," Nodding told the manuscript. Knowing Nipper, it would make good reading.

He slid the papers onto his bedside table and turned off the light,

"Wow," he whispered. Christmas Eve had turned into the high point of his life. Nodding realized he was deeply happy. He smiled in the darkness and felt a tear roll down his cheek.

Beyond the beach, deep in the cold dark water, a pulsing green light grew brighter, answering the flashing blue star at Stillwaters.

It was Christmas!

Wyatt Retired

by
Floyd "Nipper" Eisenhower

James O. Weeks

1882 – Iron Springs, Arizona

With the posse slowly trailing behind him, Wyatt Earp swung off his horse, holding the shotgun in his right hand. The horses were tired and thirsty, and the water hole would be a welcome rest. He turned and saw Doc Holiday and Jack Vermilion following closely, looking tired.

As he reached the top of the knoll above the spring, Wyatt saw nine cowboys cooking over a small, smokeless fire. These were the men who had killed his brother Morgan, the men his posse had been chasing.

As he saw the posse, Curly Bill Brocius turned and fired a shotgun at Wyatt. He had hurried, and his shot was wide, only ripping into Earp's coat.

Wyatt raised his 10 gauge shotgun and fired both barrels at Curly Bill, hitting him in the chest, knocking him into the water. Wyatt fired again at the cowboys as the posse rode up beside him.

As the cowboys scattered, shooting, the posse opened fire. Wyatt dropped the shotgun, pulled a pistol and fired, hitting an outlaw in the chest. A bullet hit his boot heel, while another ripped into his saddle horn.

Then the firing stopped. No one in the posse had been injured.

Pulling up his gun belt, he swung into the saddle. The chase was over.

1920 – Vidal, California

"I'm walking over to the post office," Josie said, tying her bonnet. "This would be a good time to sweep the floor." She pointed at the broom, leaning against the kitchen wall.

She opened the door and looked back. "And if Bart shows up, there's enough chicken in the icebox."

Wyatt Earp put down his coffee cup. "I swept the floor yesterday," he said to the empty room. "And he hates the name Bart. You're the only one who ever uses it."

He heard the locomotive whistle as it started to leave the Vidal station. Without the station and post office, the town would die. Wyatt thought it might crumble soon anyway.

He walked to the door and stepped out onto the porch, intending to sit in one of the rocking chairs, but he stopped as he saw the man limping down the road towards him.

"I say, old timer," the man said, waving his cane. "Is this the town where Wyatt Earp, the famous lawman, is in seclusion?"

"Just who wants to know?" Wyatt said, smiling and stepping forward.

"I do," the man said. "William Barclay Masterson, news reporter from New York City."

"Good to see you, Bat." Wyatt shook Masterson's hand. "I heard you had yourself a newspaper job back east. You like it?"

"I'm a sports writer," Masterson said. "I see a lot of action that way, and no one has shot at me of late."

"At least not yet," Wyatt said. He took Masterson's bag and led the way into the house. He glanced at the kitchen broom, but left it alone.

"New York does not take kindly to guns," Masterson said. "City cops arrested me twice for carrying a concealed pistol. Now they watch for me, so I stopped carrying it."

"I keep my pistol in a drawer, in case of rattlers. Hell, I don't even own a holster no more. Besides, I can't hit anything." Wyatt shrugged. "I guess times change."

"Not necessarily. That's why I'm here, Wyatt. But that can wait. I know Josie won't allow whiskey anymore, but I'm thirsty."

"I have cold tea and buttermilk," Wyatt said. His icy blue eyes waited.

"Tea would be wonderful," Masterson said. "You take stock in those rumours of prohibition? That will change social life a goodly bit."

"Next year," Wyatt said, handing Bat a glass of tea. "That's one of the reasons Josie and I came here after running saloons for thirty years. We own a little mine and some oil wells. Ain't as much money as with a saloon, but they ain't gonna outlaw gold or oil. We stay here until summer, when it's just too hot. Besides, I'm seventy, and I don't have the energy I used to."

"Think you could handle a little adventure?" Bat winked at him. "You aren't that old. I'm heading into a bit of a mystery, if you'd like to join me."

"Don't own a horse, and I don't know how to drive a car. But of course I'm up for anything."

"We can take the train into Los Angeles. After that, a streetcar will get us where we need to be." Bat looked across the table at Wyatt. "Remember the boxer who beat Jack Dempsey?"

"Gentleman Jim Corbett."

"I got to know him back then. A real decent young man. He's out here right now, getting small roles in movies."

Bat drained the tea and put down his glass. "Two days ago I was in Reno, doing an interview. I got a telegram from Corbett saying there was something bad going on, and he didn't trust the police. I said I would help and hopped a train. But I need a hand to get around those movie lots, and I could use someone I trust with me."

"I'll have to persuade Josie to let me go," Wyatt said.

"Go where?" Wyatt's wife pushed the door open and came in. "I could hear you boys talking out by the road."

She pulled her bonnet off and hung it next to the door before coming into the kitchen.

Bat stood and smiled at her. "Good to see you, Josie. It's been quite some time."

"More than thirty years. I see you shaved your upper lip, Bart."

"Smooth faces are the style in New York," he said. "Care to take a seat?"

Bat pulled back the empty chair next to him, and remained standing as Josie took a seat at the table.

"Now," she said, "what are you boys planning?"

"Bat would like to see the movie lots and can introduce me to Gentleman Jim Corbett," Wyatt said. "But it means spending the night in Los Angeles."

"Will there be drinking?"

"None is planned," Bat said. "Would you like to come with us, Josie?"

"Good heavens, no. Wyatt loves the cowboy pictures and spends time where they're filmed. I've had enough horses and smelly men for a lifetime. But you boys go right ahead."

"You don't mind?" Wyatt said.

"Not at all. I won't be here myself. Jenny invited me to a women's prohibition meeting in Ogden, Utah."

She looked at Bat and lowered her voice. "Not every soul in Utah is Mormon."

"When are you going?" Wyatt said. "You can take the train to the city with us in the morning."

"The train east doesn't leave until mid-afternoon." She stood. "I'll be fine, Wyatt. Now you start planning dinner while I get packed."

Wyatt mixed some black beans and corn together and heated some tortillas. Outside in a little fire pit, he burned some dry wood down to coals, then grilled chicken parts over them.

"Josie might eat some chicken," he said, "but usually she sticks with vegetables. As for me, this meal would be helped along with a cold beer."

"I imagine we can find some in Los Angeles," Bat said. "I reckon I'm a lucky man, Wyatt. Emma loves a drink now and then. Always has."

"What about prohibition?" Wyatt said, turning the chicken.

"There is plenty of alcohol if you know where to look. That chicken smells damned good."

Josie ate beans and corn, so Wyatt and Bat split the chicken. It was cooked nicely and tasted delicious with the fresh corn.

After the meal, Wyatt washed their dishes. Then he got extra blankets and a pillow out for Bat and made up a bed on the daven-port. The train to Los Angeles left at seven-thirty in the morning, so they all went to bed promptly.

~

The next morning the men were up early. Wyatt brewed a pot of coffee while Bat washed up. Then Wyatt washed and put on his black suit, the one with the special pocket inside the coat.

Josie was still sleeping, so he quietly opened a drawer in the table next to the davenport and removed his pistol.

"That's an antique," Bat said softly. "Still shoot okay?"

"I hope so," Wyatt said. "Shot in the air a few times in Alaska to warn off a bear. Worked then. That's as exciting as life up there got in our little town."

He slipped the gun into his special pocket. "Had this kind of pocket sewn into coats ever since Tombstone. A lot better than sticking it in my belt."

He slipped into the bedroom and said goodbye to Josie. He came back out and he and Bat drained their coffee mugs, then walked over to the train station, each carrying a small valise with a change of clothes. No ticket agent worked the station, so they stood next to the tracks where the engineer would see them.

The train was on schedule, so within fifteen minutes they were in the coach and on their way.

"Tickets?" the conductor said, stopping beside them. Wyatt reached for his wallet, while Bat flashed a badge.

"Federal marshal," the conductor said. "Then your trip is on the government, sir." He looked at Wyatt. "Is this your prisoner?"

"Not a chance," Bat said. "This gentleman is Wyatt Earp."

"My gracious," the conductor said. "It's an honor to have you with us, gentlemen. Mr. Earp, your ride is on the Union Pacific Railroad." He smiled and moved on.

"You're still a lawman?" Wyatt said. "That badge looked official."

"Oh, it is. President Roosevelt named me, Luke Short, and some others as marshals for New York. But the city police don't recognize it, so it's all a political stunt. I still can't carry a pistol."

"Interesting. This trip will take us about three hours, so there's plenty of time to get caught up on what we're doing."

"So how did you get to know the cowboys in the movies?" Bat said, lighting a cigar.

"I went to meet a young director, a guy named John Ford. He invited me to come back anytime to let the boys know what it was really like back then. So, I go back now and then. I know Tom Mix and Bill Hart and others. Ford invites me over to his house, and we have a few drinks. It's a good time." Wyatt looked out the window.

"You don't go to the movies," Bat said. "Any more that I do. We know it wasn't pretty when men got shot. Hell, even I got shot." He puffed on his cigar. "So what made you go meet this Ford fellow?"

"When I meet people and they hear my name, all they think of is the OK Corral. They know I hunted down the men who killed Virgil and Morg and shot them down in fair fights. But after that, I couldn't get a job as a lawman, no matter what good I had done in the past." He looked at Bat. "I want them to make a movie to tell how it really was."

"What does Ford say?"

"He says silent movies are all about action and not good at telling about people and their motives."

"So, no luck?"

"Not yet," Wyatt said. "But he says talking movies are coming soon, and then they could make the movie I want to see made."

"How long is 'soon'?"

"Don't know. So I go back from time to time. They're good fellows, and I hope on some visit I'll hear good news."

They rode in silence for a while. Masterson closed his eyes and dozed, while Wyatt watched the dry brush as the train moved north. When he was younger, he'd travel with his horse in the baggage car. He'd have a few drinks with the baggage clerk, who was happy for the company and protection.

But now train robberies were almost unheard of, and saddle horses were rarely seen in towns, let alone cities. It was a new world, one of streetcars, automobiles, and soon, no more bars or saloons.

Wyatt thought that might cause problems for folks, and he was interested to see how it worked out. Bars were popular everywhere, so where would the drinkers spend their free time?

At least he and Bat wouldn't have to enforce the new drinking laws anywhere. Younger lawmen could have that adventure.

It was noon when the train pulled into the Union Pacific station. Wyatt led the way to a good cafe he liked, and, after a forbidden cold beer each, they ordered food. Bat chose a burrito and tamales, since New York was almost without Mexican food. Wyatt ordered a sirloin steak with fried potatoes, washing them down with a second beer.

"Now I feel human again," he said, wiping his mouth with the cloth napkin. "And I don't have to wash any dishes." He missed lunches like this where he lived. But even when they came to the city together, she wouldn't allow a beer with the meal.

He looked out at the busy street, then at Masterson. "Where do we meet Corbett?"

"He's staying at the Hollywood Hotel," Masterson said, draining his beer mug. "Gents at the newspaper said it's a classy joint."

"I reckon it is," Wyatt said. "It's close to the studios, but I usually stay at one of the smaller hotels and save a little money."

"I'll pay for the room. If I get a good story out of the trip, the paper will cover it. How do we get there?"

"We catch the streetcar right outside and ride for a spell. We can get within a block of the hotel."

They paid for lunch, carried their bags outside, and, within ten minutes, climbed onto a streetcar. It wasn't crowded in the early afternoon, so they found seats for the hour-long ride through Los Angeles. The streetcar stopped every few minutes, so their progress was slow.

The streetcar was hot, and they took off their suit coats and were still relieved to climb down and breathe the fresh air as they walked to the hotel.

The Hollywood Hotel was as fancy as any Wyatt had seen. It was also a lot larger than hotels in the boom towns he had experienced, so the elevator to the fourth floor impressed him. An elderly man sat on a stool near the doors, controlling when to stop for the passengers.

The young man who carried their bags up was polite and helpful, reminding them that the hotel had a swimming pool and outside bar, should they care to cool off. They thanked him, but chose not to try the pool. The outside bar sounded inviting, so they tipped him before he went back downstairs.

Once he had left them, they washed up and changed into fresh white shirts.

"I'm leaving my gun here for now," Wyatt said. "I saw two armed guards in the lobby, and I'd prefer they didn't shoot me by accident."

"Sounds wise," Bat said. "But by their looks, I'd be surprised if they could hit you anyway. If you're ready, let's go back to the lobby and find Gentleman Jim."

There was no sign of Corbett in the lobby, so Bat sent a message to his room, inviting him to join them in the bar before dinner. The outside bar was small and crowded, so they found a table in the bar off the lobby.

Prohibition wasn't being enforced yet, so the bar itself was crowded. They found a free table in the corner and soon were served cold beers.

"This is a far cry from that warm slop the Long Branch served in Dodge," Bat said, putting down his mug.

"Tombstone was no better. But back then it tasted just fine." Wyatt leaned forward a bit. "You ever miss them days?"

"I miss some people, but mostly I regret getting old. Limping around these days, I see people looking at me and seeing some broken old relic. They don't know about the wild times in the gambling halls, the gunfights, or the nights sleeping in the desert under the stars. That life is long gone."

"I couldn't live that way anymore," Wyatt said. "I wish I could, but times change. I have some regrets, you know, but it's too late to do things over. Hell, I have to get up to piss in the night, and my eyes are getting fuzzy. I used to be a bad pistol shot, but I suppose now I'm hopeless."

"Our gunfights are finished by now anyway," Bat said. "Can you still see where to piss and what's on your plate?"

"So far."

"That's all that matters. Here comes Corbett."

Bar patrons turned to see the large man in a dark suit strolling through the bar.

Bat stood and shook Corbett's hand, then introduced him to Wyatt. The former heavyweight was just over six feet tall, broad shouldered and handsome, with short brown hair, a warm smile, and a firm handshake.

"I can't tell you how much I appreciate you coming out here," he said, sitting down. "I spent a morning at the police station, but they weren't very helpful. Maybe it was because I was an outsider, but I got the sense they didn't really care."

"We want to hear about it," Bat said. "But let's go in to dinner and talk about it there. The meal is on me and my newspaper."

The dining room was fancy, with white linen tablecloths, expensive china, and fans along the wall keeping the large room cool. Wyatt was glad he'd changed into a clean shirt and left his Stetson upstairs. No eatery near home was this upscale. In fact, none of the boom towns he and Josie had lived in had such an establishment. There had been fine dining, but not the relaxed luxury he was enjoying tonight.

"I hear the salmon is excellent," Corbett said. "They ship it down fresh every morning from San Francisco. I just might give it a try this evening."

He was probably in his forties, Wyatt guessed, and still in solid shape. He had kept trim and fit since his heavyweight days.

The waiter arrived and Corbett gave him his choice of salmon from the leather bound menu.

"I'd like the filet, cooked rare," Bat said. "With a baked potato and creamed spinach. And melt some butter on that meat, sir. A steak with butter is true perfection. What about you, Wyatt?"

"Could I get your prime rib of beef?" Wyatt glanced at the menu. "Fairly rare would be best, with a baked potato. And I'd like a mug of cold beer to start with."

Corbett joined him in ordering a beer, but Bat chose a glass of whiskey. "I won't be able to enjoy this before long."

The drinks arrived quickly, and after a taste, Bat turned to Corbett. "What's going on that bothers you, Jim? It must be something pretty serious."

"It is. Two girls have disappeared from the movie lot. There's no sign of trouble, and they weren't even friends, so they didn't go anywhere together. They were just hopeful young girls working as extras until they got a break."

"Do you know them?" Wyatt asked.

"Never saw them," Corbett said. "But my young niece knows one. Lory's an extra, too, there on the western lot. She told the security guard, who's an ex-copper, about it. He said kids give up and quit all the time and not to worry. But she knows where one of the girls lived and went to check it. The girl had letters piled up by her door, and the dairy had delivered a quart of milk that was sour already."

"You ask any questions?" Bat said.

"Not beyond visiting the police station. The officers there were more interested in getting autographs than listening. So I telegraphed you. I don't know what else to do. I have a small part in a detective picture and I have to be on that lot, ready to jump in when they say. Besides, I wouldn't know what questions to ask or who to look for."

The meals arrived, and the men stopped talking and concentrated on their dinners. The salmon looked good to Wyatt, but his prime rib was tender and as good as he'd hoped for. It was served with some fresh horseradish, new to Wyatt, but a lively, spicy addition to his meal.

When they had finished their food and were enjoying a final drink, Wyatt returned to the missing girls.

"I know some people on the Republic lot," he said. "Bat and I can see what we can find out. Can you get word to your niece that we'll be around?"

"I'm buying her breakfast tomorrow," Corbett said. "Her name is Lory. She'll be in her bar girl dress."

"Ask her to say hello and chat," Bat said.

"We'll start out in the studio cafeteria," Wyatt said. "Good coffee and easy to talk without attracting attention."

"I'll tell her," Corbett said, standing up. "Thank you for dinner, Bat. And thank you both for looking into this."

"I hope it's nothing," Bat said, shaking Corbett's hand. "We'll touch base tomorrow." He smiled as Corbett left, then sat down to finish his drink.

"Don't sound like nothing," Wyatt said.

"It could be bad," Bat said. "But tomorrow will give us an idea."

~

After a good rest in the comfortable room, they were up at eight, clean shaven, and fresh. Wyatt checked his pistol, then slipped it into his jacket pocket before going down to breakfast.

"I heard they have corned beef hash on the breakfast menu," Bat said. "There's a good Irish diner in New York where I get it almost every morning."

"This place has a pretty impressive menu," Wyatt said. "Most folks don't have time to make a fancy breakfast, like hash. It's a treat to eat in an establishment that offers such choices."

They were led to a table next to a window and each ordered coffee.

"I noticed last night they had escargot on the dinner menu," Bat said. "Never have tried those things, even with melted butter."

"I never will. Just the thought of them slimy snails near my mouth is disgusting."

Wyatt settled for fried eggs and bacon, with a side of fried potatoes. Bat ordered the hash with eggs for himself, then took a sip of coffee.

"Suppose these girls just gave up and went home," Wyatt said. "Must happen a lot. So what makes this different?"

"Maybe they would normally tell people if they were giving up," Bat said. "I would guess living out here, even in a rooming house, is expensive if you don't have a job."

"We'll have to see how friendly these extras are with each other. Maybe Jim's niece just didn't hear helpful news about them."

The waiter delivered their meals then, and both men concentrated on their food. Wyatt admired Bat's hash, but his bacon was thick and crisp, and he enjoyed his breakfast thoroughly.

1876 – Sweetwater, Texas

Army Scout Bat Masterson lingered as men left the Sweetwater Dance Hall and the manager turned off the lamps. Soon the hall was empty except for Bat and a young woman,

Mollie Brennan, the lead dancer, sat next to him in the front row. "I'm glad you enjoyed the show, Mr. Masterson," she said, smiling. "And thank you for staying behind with me."

"My pleasure," he said. "And please call me Bat. It's a nickname I've grown used to."

"I shall," she said. "I asked you to remain because I'm a bit nervous about one of the soldiers. He's been a regular member of the audience for over a week and has begun bringing me flowers."

"It sounds as though you have an admirer."

"I'm used to that, but he seems to believe I feel the same way. He told me he wouldn't allow me to see other gentlemen and was angry when I had him shown out of the theater. So I'm fearful about being alone just now."

"I'm more than happy to remain here with you and then escort you home when you're ready," he said.

"Thank you so much," she said, squeezing his arm. "If you're willing, you could help me out in my dressing room." She kept her hand on his arm and smiled.

Bat stood and followed Mollie through a curtained archway and down a hallway to a closed door.

"Come right in," she said, opening the door.

"You harlot," a man in her dressing room said. He was in an army uniform and raised a pistol aimed at Masterson.

"Stop, Anthony," she said, stepping through the door, her arms stretched out, but he fired the gun and Mollie collapsed, shot in the heart.

"No," he screamed, raising the pistol and firing at Masterson. His face was twisted in rage.

Bat felt the bullet hit his hip, but by then his gun was out and raised. He fell back from the doorway, but he fired twice, killing Anthony Clarke.

1920 – Hollywood, California

After a stop at the men's room, Wyatt and Bat took a streetcar to within a block of the Republic studio. At the gate, the guard let them in at once, telling Wyatt he was glad to see him back.

"Lou's a cowboy fan," Wyatt said. "Let's make his day."

He paused at the gate and shook the guard's hand. Then he introduced Lou to Bat, and Bat gave him a signed business card before they headed for the cafeteria.

"Now you can come and go as much as you want," Wyatt said. "Just in case we don't want the western production lot to know we're here."

They walked the short distance to the studio cafeteria, taking it slowly so Bat wouldn't strain his weak leg. They paused before heading in.

"Let's play it by ear," Bat said. "See what she tells us."

"Sounds good to me," Wyatt said. "We'll get some coffee and find a table. Two old guys should be easy for her to spot."

He got to the door, then paused. "I miss this feeling. You don't know what's beyond the door. Could be friends, could be danger. You have to open the door and face it."

"You're a bit of a romantic," Bat said, reaching for the door. "This is how I got shot, and I don't miss it."

"But suppose he had missed." He smiled and waited for Bat to open the door.

"He didn't," Bat said, pulling open the door.

In the large room there were quite a few empty tables. The cafeteria line was at the back of the room, so Wyatt headed there for coffee while Bat found them a table near a window. They would be easy to see by anyone entering the cafeteria.

Wyatt got the coffee and took the mugs to the table, where he saw a young lady in her early twenties sitting with Bat. She was dressed in costume as a western bar girl, with long, thick brunette hair framing her pretty face.

"Wyatt, say howdy to Lory Corbett," Bat said. He nodded as Wyatt put down the coffee mug. "She and Jim finished breakfast early, so he could get to his set."

"It's a pleasure," Wyatt said, sitting down across from Lory. "Are you working on the new Tom Mix picture?"

"I'm only an extra, Mr. Earp," she said. "I'm always in the background of the saloon, but it's my first job so I can't complain. And it's been a lot of fun."

"When does the filming end?" Bat said.

"Probably next week at the latest. They're shooting outdoor action scenes this morning, because the weather is clear."

"What then?" Wyatt asked. "A comedy? Detective picture?"

"I have a better chance with westerns," Lory said. "I have long hair, and the modern movies want girls with shorter hair, to be in style. I hear John Ford will be shooting a picture later this month. Tom Mix is finishing this one ahead of schedule."

"Your uncle said you were concerned about a friend?" Bat said.

"Judy Finck. She didn't show up on the lot for two days, so I went by her apartment. Her neighbor said she hadn't been around for a couple of days. She just vanished."

"Maybe she just gave up and went home," Bat said, putting down his mug.

"Not Judy. She had a part-time job as a cashier at a theater in the evening. She was making enough to get a cheap apartment. Most of us live on what the studio pays, so we stay in boarding houses."

"How about a boyfriend?" Wyatt said.

"Oh, she had one. Her Tommy. Judy was nuts about him. She introduced him to the gang a couple of months ago."

"Think he might know anything?" Wyatt leaned forward a bit.

"No chance," Lory said. "He's a sailor boy, and he's out in the Pacific somewhere for at least another month. Judy could hardly wait for him to get home. She thought he might propose to her. But there's more than just Judy. A girl named Holly disappeared the same way, just before I got hired. I never met her, but she had been staying in the boarding house where I live. The girls said she seemed happy, then just didn't come home one night."

"Do many of the girls you know work on your lot?" Bat said.

"No. Only two of us are in this picture. Most of the girls in the boarding house work in the police pictures or the comedies. Now that's just extras, of course. The major actresses don't have anything to do with us."

"Tell you what," Bat said. "You go ahead and do what you normally do. Wyatt and I will wander around and chat with some folks. If we can get into the set, just ignore us. We'll be back here tomorrow morning, if you want to hear what we've found out."

"Oh thank you so much," Lory said, standing up. "I'll see you tomorrow, then. I sure wish she'd turn up safe and sound."

Swishing her costume skirt, she hurried to the door.

"We can get into the set," Wyatt said. "Tom Mix is a friend of mine. He's a good kid. He loves hearing about the old days. I hear he's the top star in western pictures."

"Damn, Wyatt," Bat said. "I swear you know everyone here."

"I love watching them shoot the pictures. But it's changing, Bat. Tom Mix is building his own western set a few miles away, a whole western town. He's the number one cowboy star, so this place will miss him. John Ford will still shoot here, but he's not as famous as

Tom."

"You want Tom Mix to play you in a picture," Bat said, finishing his coffee.

"Of course I do," Wyatt said. "People respect him, and he'd do a good job. Say, there's another fellow who could play you back in Dodge City. He's a classic actor, William Hart."

"A good motion picture could help your reputation with younger folks."

"I just want people to know that we were all solid members of the community. After that OK Corral mess, it was believed we were outlaws, too. That's why Josie and I took to running saloons and gambling houses, Bat. I couldn't get any positions as a lawman."

"That's why I went to New York," Bat said. "Now they know me as a newspaperman. No more gunfighters to face or long days in the saddle."

"The buildings are a mite bigger," Wyatt said.

"But they have elevators. I admire progress like that."

"Let's progress over to the Tom Mix set. Might be good to talk to that security guard and find out what he thinks."

It took them fifteen minutes to reach the western set. As they walked, camera trucks and cars towing horse trailers passed them, back from the outdoor shoot.

"This is good," Wyatt said. "We'll see the crew and actors now. We might learn something. With this many crew members, some-one must have a clue."

They reached an open door on the side of a large building, and Wyatt led the way in. They moved over to the wall and stood quietly, observing. Men in western shirts and jeans stood around, chatting with each other.

In front of them was the interior of a western saloon, with a bar, whiskey bottles, and a large painting behind everything. In one wall of the saloon was a door to an office. Along the other side was a stairway to a balcony. Cameras and bright lights were set to film the room scenes.

A group of costumed actors came onto the set, taking their places along the bar and at two poker tables. Most were dressed as cowboys, but several men wore suits of the era.

Three young women came in and stood chatting with the men at the bar.

"There's Lory," Bat said. "She's dressed just like the other two."

"Whoever the lead actress is will be dressed nicer," Wyatt said. "They want the audience to spot her right away quick when she's on the screen."

"Wyatt Earp!" a young man in a fancy cowboy suit said, walking towards them from the door. "I didn't realize you were in town." His shirt was bright red with white fringe sewn onto each sleeve. His boot spurs jingled as he walked up to greet them.

He shook hands warmly with Wyatt, then turned to look at Bat. "Please excuse the wild shirt. It looks light grey on film."

"I hadn't planned on coming," Wyatt said. "This is my friend from wild times, Bat Masterson. Bat, meet Tom Mix."

"Golly, it's a pleasure," said Mix, taking off his hat to shake Bat's hand. His dark hair was combed in place, his white teeth gleaming in the bright light. "I'm honored you stopped in to watch. But it probably seems mighty lame compared to all the action you fellas lived through."

"There were lots of tame times, even boring ones," Bat said, smiling. "But everyone remembers the wild events."

"That's still what they want to see," Mix said. "These pictures are getting more popular all the time. I don't know if Wyatt told you, but I'm building a new western lot not too far from here. We'll have a whole frontier town to shoot in, so we won't have to keep doing our outside scenes on the edge of town."

"I heard about it," Bat said. "It should make life simpler for you."

"Say, are you living near here?" Mix said. "I'm getting a wild west show together in a few months. I keep trying to convince Wyatt to join us, but he says his wife would miss him too much. How about you?"

"Oh, I'm not too good on horseback these days," Bat said. "I live in New York. I'm out here visiting Wyatt and Gentleman Jim Corbett."

"I know Jim," Mix said. "He rides a motorcycle and so do I. But listen, they'll want me across the room in a minute. Think about a brief tour with the show, and let me know if you're interested. You don't have to ride a horse. Just stand in the ring and shoot your pistol. Even Annie Oakley uses birdshot in her guns, so she hits everything. Join us and drag this somber guy along with you! We'll all have a hot time and make some money."

Mix slapped Wyatt gently on the back and hurried onto the set.

"What's with that outfit?" Bat said. "He's a nice guy, but he'd be a target as soon as he walked into a saloon."

"Same idea as the dresses," Wyatt said, looking around the brightly lit interior. "As soon as he shows up in a scene, everyone knows the Cowboy King has arrived. But even so, he's a nice guy, a straight shooter."

"I think my western life is over," Bat said. "New York is more my style these days. It's a lot more civilized than Dodge City was. I've gotten used to a bit of luxury."

"Everything looks under control in here. If anyone tried to kidnap a young lady in plain sight, this crowd would stop him."

"A guard is stationed on the door now that it's closed," Bat said. "Let's stroll over and have a chat. At least he can let us know if he's seen anything suspicious."

They walked quietly away from the set and back to the door they had entered through. The guard was in a dark blue uniform, but he didn't have a badge. He looked to be in his fifties and was clean shaven, with receding black hair. He stepped forward when he noticed them.

As they approached, Bat pulled out his wallet and displayed his badge. "I'm a federal marshal," he said quietly. "We've been asked to look into the disappearance of a young woman who was working here."

"William Masterson?" the guard said. "Any relation to the old gunfighter I've heard about? Went by the name Wild Bill, as I recall."

"Distant relation," Bat said. "Been working here long?"

"Almost a month. Used to be on the force, but I kept getting stuck working night shifts. Here it's regular hours, which I like. But I'd rather be up on the comedy lot. Not much of a western fan, myself."

"Heard anything about a missing girl recently?" Bat said.

"Not from the studio. But one of the other actresses asked me about it. I told her people come and go around here, so I wasn't much help."

"Notice anything unusual going on the day she disappeared?" Wyatt asked. "Any strangers hanging around?"

"Can't say," the guard said. "I'm off on Thursday. You'll have to come back and talk to the man who fills in."

"What's his name?" Bat said.

"I wouldn't know. He's some young fellow Tom Mix knows. Wants to be an actor, like half of Los Angeles. I think he's working on the big set Mix is building over at Edendale. But he'll be here tomorrow, so you can ask him yourself." The guard smiled. "Unless the old folks home wants you back."

"Thanks for your help," Bat said. "There are times I wish I carried a pistol."

He led the way back to the spot they had stood in earlier. "Think it's a coincidence he has Thursday off?" Wyatt said. "It would make him an obvious suspect."

"Lory's over there," Bat said. "I'll be right back. We promised to keep her up to date."

He walked slowly over to the edge of the saloon set, where Lory was standing with two other girls. Wyatt watched Bat speaking to her, then saw her talking to the other girls. She said something to Bat, and then he came back to Wyatt.

"One of the other girls has worked here for two months," he said. "According to her, the first girl, Holly, vanished on a Thursday, too."

"That makes it more than a coincidence," Wyatt said. "Do you think watching the guard on his day off will be helpful?"

"It's our only lead so far. Let's see what we learn from watching him. We can start here tomorrow, then trace him to where he lives and take it from there."

"I'll let Tom know we'll be back tomorrow," Wyatt said. "I'll ask who we can get the guard's address from."

The actors were standing still while the crew seemed to be working on camera angles. Bat watched Wyatt chatting with Tom, then shaking his hand and coming back.

"We're all set," Wyatt said. "Tom wants to chat with us about his western town set tomorrow afternoon. They're planning a short day of filming and then taking a three-day weekend so Tom can make an appearance in Arizona. And he said he'll have all the information on the watchman for us."

"Superb. Let's go back to the hotel and enjoy the afternoon."

The set was quiet, so nothing was of great interest to Wyatt. He was ready to sit for a spell, so they re-traced their walk to the streetcar, then rode back to their hotel. It had been a while since Wyatt had been on his feet all day, and he felt it.

Once they had a chance to freshen up, Wyatt put his gun away and they went downstairs to sit by the swimming pool. Bat stopped at the desk and left a dinner invitation for Gentleman Jim.

"I realize you've probably had your fill of the sun," Bat said. "But in New York it's a bit harder to find. Tell me if you get too warm."

"The sun is fine," Wyatt said. "Josie don't care for it anymore, but I still enjoy it. But you know what would make this even nicer?"

"Aside from dancing beauties, no." Bat said. He had taken off his hat to get the sun's full effect.

"A cool pitcher of buttermilk. But I assume you'd rather have cold beer? It could build us an appetite for dinner."

"We never got around to lunch, so I concur."

Bat ordered the beer, and they spent the next two hours relaxing as they chatted about their recent lives away from Dodge City and Tombstone.

As the sun started to fade, they went upstairs, found yesterday's clothes freshly cleaned, and changed for dinner.

Gentleman Jim met them in the lobby, and they were shown to a table in the corner of the dining room. They ordered drinks, and filled Corbett in on their day. They agreed to meet in the studio cafeteria in the morning, after Jim had breakfast with Lory.

"That salmon looked good last night," Wyatt said. "We can get trout at home, but not much salmon makes it to the desert."

"My steak was delicious," Bat said, "so I'm not changing course tonight."

"I'll follow your advice, Bat," Gentleman Jim said. "I've gotten right fond of good beef in the past two years. I spent quite some time doing exhibition matches and giving speeches in the midwest cattle country."

"I visited Chicago myself," Bat said. "Baseball provided all sorts of stories."

"I'd think New York would have all the stories a newspaper could want," Wyatt said. "What with all the people."

"It wasn't a healthy place to live for a while," Jim said. "That nasty influenza was hard to avoid. So I left town when it got bad."

"As did I," Bat said, "The hotel we live in, The Chelsea, had three deaths on one floor. So we left for two months."

"Then I'm glad I live in Vidal. Heard reports of it, but damned few folks ever get off the train. We didn't have a single case of it."

The food arrived, and Wyatt was glad he ordered the salmon. Both Bat and Jim raved about their steaks, then the three were quiet as they enjoyed the meal.

"You know, I might see you gents tomorrow afternoon as well," Jim said. "Tom told me if I brought my motorcycle to the studio, he'd show me some great country roads to explore."

"Sounds like fun," Bat said. "They're getting to be quite popular."

"I agreed to go, since the missing girl issue hasn't turned up much information," Jim said. "I was hoping it would get solved quickly. I should have known better."

Wyatt looked at Bat, then shook his head. "We don't have any answers right now," he said.

"But two girls have disappeared and not been heard from in weeks. They didn't go anywhere together because they didn't know each other. And they both disappeared from the same place. Where do you think they are?" Jim said.

"Dead," Bat said. "I wager they were taken by force from that lot. If they were alive, someone would have heard something by now. Wyatt and I are going to track down the answer tomorrow, but you keep a close eye on your niece until we see you in the afternoon. Then we can watch her. But Thursday is the day to be careful."

Jim was worried, but agreed to stay close to Lory until Bat and Wyatt got to the studio in the afternoon.

~

Wyatt and Bat enjoyed a good breakfast of steak and eggs with their coffee the next morning. Wyatt tried to pay for it, but Bat insisted on putting the meal on his tab.

"New York salaries are healthier than California prices," he said. "Besides, if I get a good story out of this, then it's worth it. You have your pistol?"

"Checked this morning. Five shells and an empty chamber for carrying. But my eyes aren't that sharp anymore. I hope this won't require shooting someone."

"I agree," Bat said. "But if you're ready, let's find ourselves a streetcar."

It was another warm and sunny day, but both men wore their dark suit coats over white shirts, as much out of habit as anything. Bat wore a stylish derby, but Wyatt wore his old, flat-brimmed Stetson. The streetcar was almost empty, so the two sat comfortably.

At their stop they headed to the studio, checked in at the gate with Lou, and strolled to the cafeteria. Neither Lory nor Jim was there, so Wyatt got them coffee and they waited. They drank their coffee quietly as the tension slowly grew.

After ten minutes, Wyatt looked at Bat.

"I know," Bat said. "This isn't good."

As he spoke, the cafeteria door opened and Jim hurried in, out of breath. "I can't find Lory," he said. "She was supposed to meet me here for breakfast, but she never came. I went over to the set, but she's not there either."

"Let's go talk with Tom," Wyatt said. "We have to act fast. At least we have a place to start."

Leaving their coffee mugs on the table, they went out. Jim started to jog ahead, but Wyatt stopped him.

"Just walk," he said. "No sense in getting there out of breath. Move along, keeping your wits about you. If there's trouble ahead, you'll be ready for it."

Wyatt noticed a different guard sitting on a bench in the saloon set, looking bored. Actors and extras were slowly getting in position, while camera operators were lining up their first shots. Tom Mix was conferring with the actors when he saw Wyatt and hurried over.

"We have a serious situation," Wyatt said. He explained the missing girls and finished by filling him in on Lory's absence.

"Oh my heavens," Mix said. "We need to get the police here at once!"

"Before we do that," Bat said, "we have a possible lead." He explained that the girls had both vanished on a Thursday, which was also the security guard's day off. Finding him was a starting point for them today.

"That won't be hard," Mix said. "I asked about him yesterday afternoon. His name is Francis Ludwig, and he lives in a hotel ten blocks from here.'

"Let's go," Jim said.

"He's not there," Mix said. "He only goes there to sleep. All of his waking free time is spent in a private club in the back of a restaurant. And that's even closer. It's called the Purple Cactus Cafe. If you go back to where you catch the streetcar, turn away from the direction of your hotel. The restaurant is half a block on your left."

"What kind of place is it?" Wyatt said.

"My staff member said the food was good, but that I wouldn't like the place. He told me never to go there."

"I'm ready," Jim said.

"No," Bat said. "You ride your motorcycle to the boarding house and find out all you can. Who did she talk to, who was the last person to see her today, and anything else you can think of. We'll meet back here early afternoon."

"On my way," Jim said, and moved quickly out the door.

"We have to keep Jim away from the guard," Bat said. "He's upset and desperate, and might attack someone he thinks has hurt Lory. He could kill the man with one blow if he did, and then we'd never find Lory."

"We should be finished here by two or three, and then I can help," Mix said. "But I can break free earlier if you find her."

"Thank you, Tom," Bat said.

At the main gate, Wyatt had a word with Lou. "We're looking for Francis Ludwig. Any sign of him today?"

"Not likely I will see him," Lou said. "He never comes by on his day off. Besides, he avoids me whenever he can, on account I was on the force when he got thrown off. But I bet you can find him over at the Purple Cactus Cafe in an hour or so, once it opens."

"That's where we're headed," Bat said. "Thank you."

"I don't mean to get him fired or nothing," Lou said. "He does a good job as a guard. Not a loafer, like that young guy."

The Purple Cactus was a Mexican restaurant and social club, according to the sign outside. It was open, so they went in. A young man wearing a sombrero greeted them.

"We're looking for Francis Ludwig," Wyatt said, taking off his hat.

"Oh they're not here yet," the young man said. "They usually get here in a half hour or so. You can come back then or grab a table if you're hungry.

"We'll wait," Wyatt said. "Can we see a menu?"

"Right this way." The young man led them to a table halfway to the back. He handed them menus and said he'd be back in a moment.

"That door in the back has a 'Private' sign on it," Bat said. "The kitchen and washroom doors are back near the corner."

The young man came back with glasses of water. Wyatt ordered chicken fajitas, while Bat asked for a beef burrito. Neither asked about alcohol with the meal.

"What do you expect to find in that room?" Bat said.

"I hope they have Lory in there," Wyatt said. "Whatever it is, they want it private."

No one went into the door by the time their food arrived, but both men watched it while they ate.

"Whatever happens today will change lives," Wyatt said. "Jim, Lory, and even we will be changed."

"That's true," Bat said, taking a sip of his water.

"All of the gunfights rewrote things, but, hell, I was almost a family man in Missouri."

"Now, I didn't know that, Wyatt."

"I was married, had a little house, and my wife was pregnant. I figured I'd stay in Missouri for good. I was shaping up to be a good farmer."

"What happened to change it all?"

'Urilla took sick and died. Our baby died with her. It pretty near destroyed me for a while there. I finally left and went west to find Morgan and Virgil. But suppose our baby had lived? Or Urilla? I wouldn't be here with you now."

"We play what we're dealt," Bat said. "You ready to see what's next? It's been nearly a half hour. Don't think I'll finish this lunch." He wiped his mouth and looked back at the closed door.

"I am ready,. But something feels wrong."

"It does, but it's all we have. I'll go back. You stay here and cover the door. Stop them if they run your way."

"I have the gun," Wyatt said.

"I have a badge. If there's shooting, come running. Don't know how many are in there."

He put money on the table with their check, stood up, and walked to the rear. Wyatt put on his hat and stood up. He reached in his pocket and gripped his revolver.

The waiter appeared and took the money. "Nice hat," he said.

"You a cowboy?"

"Used to be.".

As Bat got near the door, an older man came out of the kitchen and intercepted him. Bat held out his badge and the man backed away, nodding. He led the way to the door, used a key to open it, and let Bat in.

"Does your gun still shoot?" the waiter said.

Wyatt glanced at him. "Go away," he said, and the waiter backed away. Then he turned and hurried for the kitchen.

Bat came out of the room and walked back to Wyatt. "He's not our man. Let's get out of here." He glanced back at the door, tugging his hat firmly onto his head.

He led the way to the door and stepped out onto the sidewalk.

"Did you see him?" Wyatt said. "Was he there?"

"He was there. Francis was wearing a dress and sitting on another man's lap. He's got no interest in girls."

"Damn," Wyatt said. "I wondered why there were no women in the place." He shook his head. "We need to get back to the studio and tell Jim."

"We missed something along the way," Bat said as they walked back toward the studio. "But everything pointed toward Francis on Thursday."

"We're close. There's just a piece missing somewhere."

They crossed the street to the main gate, where Lou greeted them. "Find Ludwig?" He gave them a knowing smile.

"We did," Wyatt said.

"Now you know why he got thrown off the force," Lou said. "They might fire him from here, too."

"No sense in that, if he's good as a guard," Bat said. "A man's personal life shouldn't influence his job."

"Well, like I said, he ain't lazy or always flirting with the girls like that young guy. Of course, that one's safe on account of he works for Tom Mix building that new western set. He comes and goes with Tom's horse all the time, in one of those special horse trucks. And I bet he gets paid more than me."

"Wouldn't be surprised," Wyatt said. "Thanks, Lou."

At the western set, they saw Jim's motorcycle parked outside the door. Shooting had stopped for the day, and the giant room was almost empty. They paused for a moment, looked at each other, then entered.

Jim was sitting at one of the tables, saw them, and hurried over. "Did you find him?"

"We did, but he's not our man," Bat said. "We were wrong. No sign of Lory. We're back to square one."

"Are you sure?" Jim said. "Maybe he has her hidden."

"What did you find out?" Wyatt said.

"There were three girls plus the landlady there," Jim said. "No one talked to her today. No one even mentioned seeing her."

He paused, looking at them. "Come to think of it, the landlady said she didn't see her last night, either."

Wyatt threw a glance at Bat as Tom Mix walked over to them.

"What's happening?" Tom said.

"Where's Tony?" Wyatt said. He looked at Bat, who understood.

"Who is Tony?" Jim asked.

"Back at my barn," Tom said. He looked at Jim. "Tony's my horse, Tony the Wonder Horse. They brought him back here yesterday with the other horses, by mistake. So I had Forrest come and take him home after filming yesterday."

"What do you know about Forrest?" Wyatt said.

"Not a whole lot. Wants to be a movie star, like lots of young people. He showed up without a cent, so I hired him to do some work clearing the land for Mixville. I told him he could bunk there for a while until we started using it for filming."

"Lory never got back to her boarding house last night," Wyatt said. "No one saw her leave here after Forrest drove off with a horse van."

"It's our best hope," Bat said. "He could be our man."

"Oh, no," Tom said. "He told me he'd seen a rattlesnake, so I gave him a pistol yesterday. He's got a gun if we confront him."

"We need to get there and look for Lory," Wyatt said. He looked at Tom. "Can you give us directions?"

"Even better," Tom said. "I'll pull my motorcycle to the door. Bat, you ride with Jim. I'll take Wyatt and get us there fast. We'll be there in ten minutes."

He ran to the back of the set while Wyatt, Bat, and Jim went out the front door. Wyatt helped Bat climb behind Jim on his motorcycle, a Henderson. Bat held his cane across his lap as Tom came around the building on his black Indian. He pulled a stop and nodded to Wyatt.

Wyatt checked to be sure his pistol was secure as he climbed on behind Tom, pulling his hat down firmly

"Hold tight, Wyatt," Tom said. "This runs faster than a horse. Follow me, Jim."

He gunned the cycle and they were off, with Jim following closely. Wyatt saw Lou wave as they roared through the gate and turned right.

Traffic was getting heavier, but Tom didn't seem to care, weaving between and around cars. People waved as they raced past, and Wyatt realized Tom was still in full costume, with boots, holster, and hat still firmly in place. He was a fixture in town, and tourists yearned to catch a glimpse of the King of the Cowboys.

Tom concentrated on his driving, passing two cars as he came to an intersection.

They turned onto a cross street, which was less crowded, and Tom opened the Indian up, pulling away from Jim's Henderson.

In a few minutes they swung onto a smooth dirt road, and in a half mile pulled up to a wooden gate.

Wyatt climbed off the cycle, then Tom swung off as Jim pulled up. Wyatt helped Bat climb off the Henderson as Tom stepped up to them.

"This is the end of town," he said quietly. "We'll walk down the street until we figure out where he is. I hope to God he doesn't have the girl here."

"Let's go," Jim said.

"No," Tom said. "I need you to ride back to the end of the drive, then turn right. There's a firehouse a half mile away. Stop and tell them we need the police and an ambulance. I'll open the gate as we go in."

"Don't you have a telephone?" Jim said.

"It's halfway down the street in the stable," Tom said. "If he has your niece, we can't wait until we get there. We'll need help right then."

"Got it," Jim said. He climbed back on the motorcycle, started it, and roared off.

Tom stepped up to the gate. "He's heard our cycles," he said, unlocking the gate. "Normally he'd come out to say hello. This is bad. He's in there waiting for us, and he has a gun."

"Where do you think he is?" Bat asked

"The saloon is the only building with lights and furniture so far. If he's not there, I don't know."

"As long as it's not in any corral," Wyatt said, reaching into his coat. He pulled out his pistol and handed it to Bat. "I might hit Lory."

"Let's go," Bat said, tucking the pistol into his belt. "This guy has no idea what's heading his way."

"Two old guys and a cowboy with two fake pistols," Wyatt said.

"But I have a new white hat," Tom said, grinning. "So he'll know we're the good guys."

Wyatt and Bat walked on either side of Tom, spreading out a bit to avoid making themselves easy to hit. They walked slowly, watching the false building fronts on either side of the dirt street.

"Nice little town you have here," Bat said. "But a bit quiet for my tastes."

As they neared the saloon, they slowly moved to the right, all eyes on the swinging doors.

"Stop! Please." Lory's voice was high-pitched, frightened.

"Thank God," Wyatt said. "We'll go left inside the door."

He moved ahead, closely followed by Bat, with Tom coming behind them. At the door Wyatt paused, looked back at Bat, then nodded.

They pushed through the doors and edged to the left, backs to the wall, facing the large room. Wyatt edged away from the others as they stared into the room.

Lory, in her underwear, was tied to a chair near the far end of the bar. Forrest was behind her, a revolver in his hand.

"You're just in time for the fun," Forrest said. He was still wearing his blue security uniform. "She spent last night locked up in the stable, all alone. I haven't even cut her hair or unwrapped her."

"Police are coming," Tom said. "Let her go."

"I'll hear them, just like I heard your motorcycle," Forrest said. "By the time they get here, they'll be too late." He ran a hand through Lory's hair. "But you get to watch."

"Decoy," Wyatt whispered to Bat.

Bat slid one of Tom's pistols from its holster and passed it behind his back to Wyatt, who held it at his side and stepped further to the left.

"Don't move, old man," Forrest said, putting the gun to Lory's head.

"If you shoot her, you can't stop all of us," Wyatt said, taking another step. The guard's eyes were on him now.

"I can stop you," Forrest said, pointing the gun in Wyatt's direction.

"Ever shoot at someone who can shoot back?" Wyatt said. He raised Tom's gun and shot into the air, taking another step to the left.

"That's just a blank gun," Forrest said. He aimed the gun at Wyatt, who took another step to the left.

"Is it?" Wyatt said, pointing the gun at Forrest and firing it.

Forrest flinched just a bit as he fired back, the bullet hitting the wall to Wyatt's left. Wyatt moved another step before the guard could fire again.

"Lights are in your eyes," Wyatt said. "Want another chance?" He stepped forward.

"Damn you," Forrest said, stepping away from Lory and raising the pistol. He didn't see Bat swing Wyatt's pistol up and fire. Wyatt stepped forward as Bat fired.

The old black powder revolver roared as flame and smoke shot out. Forrest screamed, dropping his pistol and grabbing his crotch before collapsing. He fell back onto the floor, away from Lory's chair.

Bat, Wyatt, and Tom rushed forward. Bat kicked the pistol away from Forrest. Wyatt took out a pocket knife and sliced the rope holding Lory to the chair. He helped her stand, draping his suit coat over her shoulders. She leaned against him and sobbed.

The sirens were coming.

"Tom," Bat said. He slid the pistol into Tom's empty holster. "You fired the shot. You saved the day."

"It was you, Bat," Tom said.

"I'm a sportswriter," Bat said. "Let everyone think Lory was saved by the King of the Cowboys."

"Help me," Forrest said, his pants covered with blood.

"Where are the other girls?" Wyatt said. He looked down and

pointed the blank gun at Forrest's head.

"Buried behind the barn," Forrest said. "I need help."

"Nice shooting, Tom," Wyatt said.

"Thank you so much, Mr. Mix," Lory said through tears. She went to him and hugged him tightly. Tom blushed and put an arm around her.

Then the saloon doors crashed open and Gentleman Jim Corbett charged into the room, stopping when he saw Lory. He started to cry. Lory turned and ran to his arms.

He was closely followed by policemen and ambulance medics, who hovered over Forrest.

"Who shot me?" Forrest said, as he was lifted onto a stretcher. "I know your gun was blanks." He looked at Wyatt.

"It was Tom Mix," Wyatt said. "He shot the rattlesnake."

There were two ambulances, one for Lory and one for Forrest. Jim followed Lory on his motorcycle, and Tom stayed with the police to search for the girls' bodies.

An officer drove Wyatt and Bat back to the hotel. He asked them to autograph his ticket book before leaving.

"I need a drink," Bat said. I'm too old for this behaviour."

They left their hats in the coat room, then went into the restaurant. Wyatt had his coat back, after Lory had been wrapped in a blanket, so he didn't feel out of place in the fancy dining room.

They were shown to a table and Wyatt ordered a mug of cold beer, while Bat wanted a shot of whiskey before their menus arrived.

Both ordered steaks, then relaxed with their drinks.

"I'm thankful for two things," Wyatt said, lifting his beer. He took a gulp and smiled as he put down the mug.

"Just two?" Bat sipped his whiskey.

"I'm thankful you can shoot straight, and I'm thankful Forrest could not."

"But my aim was off. I always say, in a gunfight, aim for the groin and you'll hit the chest. This time I hit where I aimed."

"An appropriate wound," Wyatt said. "But he deserved to die."

"He still may. All right, Wyatt, I want to ask one question before our food gets here. Why the hell did you step out and let him shoot at you?"

"I had to. We had to get him away from Lory before he hurt her. Besides, I've never been shot before. It would have been a new experience."

"If you'd been shot, Josie would have come up here and raised hell."

"I suppose that's true, but it didn't happen. Now let's enjoy this great steak." Wyatt smiled as the waiter delivered his dinner. "Tomorrow I get back to Josie's vegetarian cooking."

Both men were hungry, so there was little conversation as they ate. They passed on dessert, but each ordered a brandy to finish the dinner. They raised their glasses and toasted Jim and Lory.

After dinner, on their way to their room, Bat waited until they were leaving the coatroom with their hats. "I'm sorry I gave your gun to Tom," he said. "I think you can get it back once the police finish with it."

"I don't want it back," Wyatt said. "If I ever saw a rattlesnake, I couldn't hit the damn thing. I admit my shooting days are over."

"Mine are as well. This was a little more excitement than I want nowadays."

The next morning they brought their valises to the front desk, then had breakfast before checking out.

"Gentlemen," the desk clerk said. "Mr. Corbett has covered your charges and says he owes you everlasting thanks."

"Jim's exhibitions must pay well," Bat said. "But I still intend to write about this adventure, once the weather turns cold in New York."

"I look forward to reading it," Wyatt said. "But I don't think I'll share it with Josie. She'd never let me visit Tom Mix again. And my visits are usually pretty quiet."

"She would have been right there with us if we were in Tombstone."

"Age changes us. But she and I have been together long enough that we've changed together, almost in harmony."

"I'm glad it worked out for you," Bat said. "Now, since Jim paid for the room, I can treat us to a taxi ride to the train station."

At the station they bought their tickets. Bat was heading back to Nevada, so they were taking separate trains. Wyatt's train was due to leave shortly, so they shook hands in the terminal.

"Thank you for coming with me, Wyatt," Bat said. "I would have been lost in the studio without you."

"It was a grand adventure. Have a safe trip back to New York. Behave yourself, Bat."

Wyatt walked out to his platform, and there was Josie, waiting for her connection.

"Are you still here?" she said. "Goodness. I thought you would be home long before me, Wyatt."

"It took a little longer than I thought," he said. "How was your meeting? Was Utah a good place to gather?"

"Wonderful. I took notes, so I can tell you all about the lectures."

When their train arrived, Wyatt helped Josie up the steps and carried their bags into the car. They found seats and settled themselves.

"I, for one, cannot wait until I can enjoy the evening on our front porch," Josie said. "I missed hearing the coyotes howling under those bright stars."

"Suppose," said Wyatt. "Suppose the trading post has some fresh buttermilk?"

1921 – Vidal, California

It was mid-morning in late October in Vidal. The summer heat had died down, and Wyatt and Josie Earp had moved back to their house after a summer in Los Angeles. The desert was peaceful, which Wyatt was enjoying after the bustle and noise of the city.

He was in a rocking chair on the front porch, watching Josie stroll back from the trading post. She was bringing groceries and the mail, including a day-old newspaper from the city. He stood as she reached the porch, taking the bag of groceries from her. He turned to take them into the house.

"Wyatt, wait," she said. "There's a telegram here for you. It's from Tom Mix. Maybe they're doing a picture about you. They've been talking about pictures with sound for so long."

She handed the envelope to Wyatt, who put the bag of groceries down on the rocker before opening the telegram and reading it silently.

"Damn," he finally said. "It's bad news, Josie. Bat Masterson died the other day in New York."

"Good grief. He was just here last year."

"That's why Tom sent the telegram. He got to know Bat when we went to the studio. Says Bat died of a heart attack at the newspaper office. He just collapsed without any warning."

"Oh, I'm sorry, Wyatt," she said, squeezing his arm. "You two were such good friends before I ever met you."

"Most of my Tombstone friends are long gone. First Morgan,

then Doc and Virgil. But I knew Bat from back in my Dodge days. Makes a man feel mighty lonely."

"I know, Wyatt," she said. "And there's no good friend around here to talk to, either. Tell you what. I need you to bring home a bag of potatoes I bought up at the store. I know Ruby has some of that bootleg beer hidden away. I don't suppose a bottle of that could hurt you. You could drink a toast to Bat."

"You always called him Bart," Wyatt said, reaching for his hat.

"I did that to needle the two of you, but it doesn't feel right to do it now. Maybe I'll write his wife a letter tonight."

On his way down the dirt road to the train tracks and trading post, Wyatt kicked a stone along in front of him, watching it stir up dust as it bounced. Summer was over, but it was still hot on the edge of the desert. He was glad he didn't have to spend his days inside the windowless store.

He crossed the railroad tracks and saw a Ford parked next to the store with a man and woman inside. Wyatt didn't recognize the car. He couldn't make out the people until the driver's door opened.

As he got closer, Sheriff Roy Gardner stepped out and hurried to meet him. He was a short, wiry man in his sixties, wearing a white uniform shirt and brown pants. "Wyatt, thank God you're here. Ruby flagged me down as I was driving in to get the mail."

"What's up?"

"There's a young man inside with a gun," the sheriff said. "Ruby was in the stock room when he came in, so she skedaddled right out the back. She has a pistol under the front counter, but of course, she wasn't anywhere near it."

"How can I help?" Wyatt said.

"Just keep an eye on the front. I'll go around back and sneak in that door. If he comes out, don't try to stop him, but let me know where he goes."

"I can do that." The sheriff nodded, slapped his pistol in its holster, and turned to the rear of the building.

Wyatt watched the sheriff move quietly towards the back of the building. "But I won't."

He went directly to the front porch and opened the door to the trading post. A young man in his late teens stood at the counter.

"Hands up," the young man said, stretching his arm out to point the revolver at Wyatt. "Do you work here?"

"No. I'm Wyatt Earp. Now give me that gun." Wyatt stepped toward the young man and held out his hand.

"Yessir," the boy said, handing the gun to Wyatt. "I wouldn't shoot anyone. I just wanted some food."

Wyatt took the pistol, opened the cylinder, and took out the three bullets he found. He slipped them into his pocket.

"If Sheriff Gardner had come in and seen you with this gun, he would have shot you. Now don't say anything stupid."

Wyatt put the pistol on the counter and turned to the back of the store. He heard a door shut. "It's all clear, Sheriff," he said loudly.

Another door in the back opened and the sheriff came into the room, holding his pistol.

"This young fella was bringing in the pistol to sell to Ruby," Wyatt said. "I checked it, and it's empty."

"That so?" the sheriff said, putting his pistol back in its holster as he stepped forward. "Young man, you could have been killed."

"I know," the boy said. "I'm sorry."

"What's your name?" the sheriff said, picking up the pistol and opening the cylinder. "This gun needs a cleaning."

"Andrew Click," the boy said. 'I just moved in with my grandmother about two miles south of here."

"Your grandmother Marsha Click? How's she doing?" the sheriff relaxed a bit and shook the boy's hand.

"She's having a little trouble with her memory, so I said I'd come give her a hand. She insists on living alone out here. I thought I could help by staying with her."

"You walk over today?" The sheriff looked at the boy's worn clothing.

"Yessir," the boy said, glancing at Wyatt. 'We needed some food.".

"Reason I asked," the sheriff said, "Ruby gets a truck in here once a week. It's too much to unload and stock it all by herself. I bet she'd be willing to trade some supplies if you could come in and help."

"I'd be happy to help."

"She's sitting out in my car," the sheriff said. "I'll go explain the gun and mention it. Thanks for your help, Wyatt. This turned out better than I thought it would."

He opened the front door and stepped onto the porch.

"Thank you," the boy said. "You kept me from destroying my life."

"Or ending it," Wyatt said.

He pulled out a worn wallet and handed the boy a ten dollar bill. "In case she won't buy the gun. I gave my last pistol away a year ago, and I was thinking about that on my way over here. It solved a lot of situations, but it also led to heartbreak. Don't take that path, son."

The door opened and Ruby stepped in, looking relieved. She smiled, nodded at Wyatt and relaxed.

"Josie sent me for potatoes," Wyatt said.

"Down at the end of the counter," Ruby said, pointing at a large bag. She looked at Andrew. "And I understand you have a gun you're offering for sale?"

"Yes ma'am. It's empty and needs a good cleaning, but I didn't know how." He nodded to the gun, sitting on the counter where Wyatt had left it.

"Just as well," Ruby said, stepping behind the counter.

"I'll be heading home," Wyatt said, picking up the potato sack.

He opened the door.

"Thanks, Wyatt," Ruby said. "Sorry for the confusion." She picked up the revolver and opened it.

"Thanks again, Mr. Earp," Andrew said.

Wyatt nodded, pulled his hat a bit lower, and stepped out. He slung the bag of potatoes over his shoulder and strolled back to his home.

"No beer?" Josie said when he got in the house.

"Clean forgot," Wyatt said. "I guess buttermilk will do just fine."

"Brent stopped by with a bag of ore," she said. "He says the gold is still slow and steady, but he was chipping away at a side wall and swears he found some silver tracings."

"That's unusual for this area. But if Brent thinks so, we should get it checked. I'll have to get it assayed."

"What if there is some silver and word gets out?" Josie said. "We don't want all kinds of fools charging in and disturbing our mine. And you know they will."

"It seems like word gets out," he said.

"People around here can't keep their big mouths shut. I know it's a chore, but I think you need to hop on the train and ride the ore sample over to Phoenix. If they don't know you, no one will connect it to our mine."

"I suppose it makes sense. But folks know me in Phoenix from our saloon days. I'll go to Prescott, which barely existed back then."

"Now pour yourself some buttermilk," Josie said. "You can get packed after dinner. You'll have to stay a night or two."

~

Wyatt caught the southbound train the next morning. It was a hot ride across the dry flats, but he got to Prescott without incident by mid-afternoon. It was a busy little town and he quickly spotted several hotels and the assay office.

It was a boom town like them all, sprawling out with temporary shacks and tents from a small cluster of established wooden buildings. The hotels, diners, and assay office were located near each other in the older wooden buildings.

Wyatt saw a decent hotel near the assay office, where he stopped to drop off his ore sample. He used the name Barry Stamp, his middle names, for privacy. He knew using Earp in a town like this would cause rumors and speculation.

Then he walked over to the Susquehanna Hotel and registered under the same name.

"Going to be in town long?" the clerk, a short, stocky man, asked. A few of the room keys were missing, but the hotel was far from full.

"Two nights," Wyatt said. "Do you serve meals here?"

"Used to, in the dining room. But without liquor the food makes no money, so we rent out the space to a women's clothing store. Across the street the LaHave Bakery serves mighty tasty food. They have beef, of course, but the best dinner is the chicken. I recommend it to all our guests, Mr. Stamp."

Wyatt thanked him and went upstairs to his room on the second floor. It was a far cry from the hotel he had shared with Bat in Los Angeles. There was no elevator or fancy dining room here, but his room was clean and had electricity, so he didn't have to bother with an oil lamp.

After hanging his suit jacket in the wardrobe, Wyatt freshened up and then went across the street for an early dinner. He was ready for a tasty meal without drama. His biggest choice would be a cold drink with the meal.

The chicken was as good as promised, and Wyatt enjoyed a glass of cold buttermilk with the meal. He chose to bypass the chocolate cake for dessert, paid for his meal, and walked back to the hotel.

The street was still busy, but Wyatt was ready for a good night's sleep.

Passing through the lobby, he noticed a young man standing in the dress shop, looking out of place. The same young man was there who had been on duty when Wyatt went out for dinner. Years of experience had prepared him for situations like this.

Wyatt thought the hotel was too small to employ a Pinkerton guard, so when he got to his room he left his door ajar and stood looking out the window.

"Raise your hands." The voice was young and nervous.

The young man stepped into the room, holding a pistol. Wyatt turned slowly and saw the badge on the white shirt.

"Come in," Wyatt said. The officer was in his early twenties, with a tanned face. His eyes darted around the room nervously, and Wyatt realized he was blushing.

"Don't you make any sudden moves," the young man said.

"The room is too small for that, and I do not plan to jump out of the window." Wyatt made the young man smile, which was a start.

"I was informed you were violent and would not be taken alive."

"If that were true, you should not have braced me alone. You could have been killed, son."

"You're forgetting that I am holding the gun, sir"

Holding the gun ain't the same as firing it," Wyatt said. "First, that gun isn't fully loaded. I can see that from here. Second, you have the safety on. You'd have to pull back the hammer before firing. By that time, someone with a pistol would have put several bullets into you. So put the gun down and tell me why you're here."

The young man lowered the pistol, but didn't put it in his holster. "A resident of Prescott has formally charged you with making threats on her life and business."

"Who is this woman?" Wyatt said.

"Mrs. Howard. She owns a boarding house up the street. She

says you wrote her a threatening note yesterday."

"On the bureau next to you is my wallet. Folded in it is my railroad ticket to and from Prescott. It should clearly demonstrate that I only arrived in town this afternoon. The desk clerk can also testify to that fact."

The young man slipped his pistol into its holster and picked up the wallet. He removed the train ticket and read it, then nodded. He opened the wallet, looked at Wyatt's California Voters Card, then looked back at Wyatt, blushing.

"Oh God," he said. "I pulled a gun on you, sir."

"I'm here somewhat secretly. That's why the desk clerk knows me by a different name," Wyatt said.

"Gosh. I never thought to check with him. I just followed you after Mrs. Howard pointed you out before dinner."

"Just how long have you been a deputy?"

"Three months as of Sunday," the young man said. "I'm still on probation with the chief. I hope to make my first arrest soon."

"Well, son, you know my name. What's yours?"

"Jed Davis, sir."

"I thought you looked familiar. Any kin to Ridge Davis, the saddle maker?"

The young man straightened up and smiled. "He's my father. My family lives over in Phoenix."

"I knew him when he was just starting out in Tombstone," Wyatt said. "He's one to ride the river with, a good man."

"Yes he is."

"Well, Jed Davis, I need to talk with Mrs. Howard to find out why she thinks I'm the one threatening her. And then I suppose we need to find whoever that person is and put a stop to it."

"Right."

"The police might have to be involved at the end," Wyatt said. "Can we work as partners on this?"

"Oh gosh, of course," Jed said. "Yes, sir."

"Fine," Wyatt said. "Let's meet at nine tomorrow morning at the cafe across the street. But before we meet, you need to fill in your chief, so he knows you might resolve this complaint."

He shook hands with Jed, who then left. With the room finally quiet, Wyatt got undressed and climbed into bed.

Outside, the street noises continued until almost midnight. This was a small town, but a lively one.

He finally dozed off, still curious about who Mrs. Howard was and why she complained about him.

The street was busy again by seven-thirty, filled with automobile sounds, voices calling, and still an occasional horse. Wyatt was already awake and crossed the street to the cafe at eight.

He enjoyed a breakfast of bacon and eggs with hot biscuits and was on his second cup of coffee when Jed Davis came into the cafe with a blond man in his forties, wearing a white shirt, badge, and holstered pistol. Wyatt stood to greet them.

"Mr. Stamp, it's an honor to meet you," the chief said. "I'm Walker Steele."

Wyatt smiled at the chief's use of his alias.

He and Wyatt shook hands, and Wyatt offered them seats and ordered coffee for them. He was impressed that they had checked the hotel register before coming to the cafe.

"I see you've found the best food in town," the chief said. "Been to Prescott often?" He smiled at the waiter and sipped his coffee.

"Passed through years ago, when this was just a village. This trip was to quietly visit the assay office with a sample from our mine. I hope to catch a morning train back to Vidal first thing tomorrow."

"Officer Davis says you don't know anything about this threat to Mrs. Howard," the chief said, sipping his coffee.

"I don't even know who she is," Wyatt said. "Though she apparently knows me. I asked Officer Davis to introduce me today, so we could straighten this all out."

"Well, she's new to town herself," the chief said. "I've met her husband, John Howard, who owns a small mine near here. They've started running a boarding house up the street, which all seems on the up and up. I'll be interested in what you find out."

"I'm sure I've made some enemies in the past, but Josie and I travelled down to California from Alaska and Oregon. We ran saloons and gambling houses, but retired when Prohibition was being passed. So if someone here has a grudge, it's more than thirty years old."

"Well, sir, we'll help in any way we can. I appreciate you working with Jed, here. Let me know if I can be of any further help. Thank you for the coffee."

The chief stood up, shook Wyatt's hand, patted Jed on the back, and left the cafe.

"Ready to go find her?" Jed said, draining his coffee mug. "I see her a lot at the dress shop in the hotel dining room. I think she works there."

"Charging into a scene isn't the smart way to proceed," Wyatt said. "I prefer to observe first, so I know what I'm likely to find."

"That makes sense."

"For example, I watched you and your chief stop at the hotel before walking over here. He had you wait outside while he stepped inside. That way no one would come in and take him by surprise."

"How did you figure he was the chief?"

"His gun," Wyatt said. "Most officers in this part of the country carry revolvers, like you. Your chief carries one of those Browning Model 1911 pistols. They're still too expensive for most departments to issue, so I figured he would be the chief."

"Wow," Jed said. "So how do we proceed?"

"Let's stroll over to the dress shop. If she knows me, I suppose I'll recognize her. I assume she'll be angry at me, so let's keep the meeting calm."

Wyatt paid the check, pulled on his flat-brimmed hat, and stepped out of the cafe. Out of habit he paused and looked both ways before crossing the street.

A truck drove by, and then he and Jed crossed the street and stepped into the hotel. He nodded at the desk clerk, then turned and went into the dress shop. Jed slid back a bit, letting Wyatt lead the way.

An older woman had her back to them, but turned as Wyatt removed his hat.

"Have you arrested him yet?" she said, glaring at Jed. She finally shifted her eyes to Wyatt.

"Hello, Kate," Wyatt said. "I didn't realize you lived here. It's been a long time since Tombstone."

"Then why did you send me that threat?"

"He didn't," Jed said. "Mr. Earp wasn't even in town until you saw him checking in. This is a case of mistaken accusation."

"Nonsense," she said. "No one in town knows me from my past. No one else dislikes me. How else can someone make threats?"

"Kate, we had a disagreement over thirty years ago. It's high time we left it in the past. I don't dislike you and would never make any threats against you. Most everyone from back then has passed."

"You and your brothers all were angry."

"Officer Davis, we're talking about issues that should not be shared beyond this room. But you need to know why someone might make threats against Kate, so you can protect her safety after I leave for home."

"I understand," Jed said.

"Mrs. Howard used to keep company with one of my good friends, John Holliday. There was some friction between the women to start with."

"Doc Holliday?" Jed said. "Wow."

"We had some ups and downs," Kate said. "But I loved him."

"At one of those down points, some corrupt men got Kate inebriated and tricked her into signing a statement accusing Doc of holding up a stage. It all worked out, but there were some ill feelings created."

"Your brothers hated me," Kate said.

"Doc forgave you," Wyatt said. "So I forgave you. Besides, they're all gone now."

"I was with Doc when he died," said Kate. "You never loved anyone long enough to be there when they passed. You got tired of Mattie and just threw her aside when Josie came along."

"That's not the whole story, Kate," Wyatt said. There's always more to a story."

"It's what Mattie told me."

"Mattie was addicted to laudanum. She took money from me to buy it, then stole to buy it, and finally started whoring to buy it. She wasn't the same person."

"So you cast her aside," Kate said.

"No. I sent Maddie with my brothers' families to California. But she wouldn't stay with them when I didn't show up. She went back to whoring and then died of an overdose."

'You never cared enough to stay with her," Kate said. "Do you even know what love really is?"

Wyatt sighed, looked at Jed briefly, and nodded. "Yes I do, Kate. Before I met you and Doc, I lived in Missouri. I was in love, married, and happy back there. My wife caught the fever and died in childbirth. I fell apart afterwards, and the only thing that saved me was family. They told me to come west and join them. I did, and they cured my broken life. I prayed they could do the same for Mattie, but she wouldn't let them. That's when I met Josie, and we've been together ever since. So I do know, Kate."

"I didn't realize, Wyatt. I'm trying to get on with my life, too. I'm married to a good man who knows my past and loves me anyway. We've come here for a fresh start, to run an honest boarding house. Then someone wrote me a threatening note and slipped it under the door at night. When I saw you, I figured it had to be you who wrote it. I don't know who else would know my past enough to make threats."

"Just what did this note say?" Jed asked.

Wyatt nodded at his attempt to tackle the issue at hand.

"It said, 'We know you, Big Nose. Put your house up for sale and leave town. First we'll put your story in the newspaper, then send news about your sporting house to the saloons. If you're still here, we'll burn you out.'"

"We can't let that happen," Jed said.

"We won't," Wyatt said. "Jed and I will figure this out this afternoon, I hope. Did you tell your husband about the note?"

"No. John went out to his mine the day before it showed up. He's not due back until the day after tomorrow."

"Then he can't help us," Jed said.

"Come to think of it, John said a man approached him at the post office a few days back," Kate said. "He asked about buying the boarding house and was pushy about it."

"Did your husband know him?" Wyatt said.

"John had never seen him. But he told him no, because it is all in my name anyway. And that was that."

"That's where we'll start," Wyatt said. "We'll be back."

He stepped out through the lobby and onto the wooden sidewalk. Jed closed the door behind them.

Jed followed him out to the street, where Wyatt took a moment to pull his hat onto his head, providing a little shade from the blazing Arizona sun.

"What do you think?" he said.

"Well, I think it's a coincidence that someone wanted to buy the boarding house before the note showed up," Jed said.

"I agree. So how can we find out more? We need details to solve the case Where do we look?"

"We need to learn who the man was."

"How do we do that?"

"Well," Jed said, "we should check the town hall and see if anyone asked there about the property."

"But then he'd learn only Kate's name was listed," Wyatt said. "How would he know to ask John Howard?"

Jed thought for a moment while Wyatt surveyed the street. "Someone at the post office must have pointed Mr. Howard out."

"Good point," Wyatt said. "Let's take a stroll down there."

They walked to the post office, about a block away. Wyatt sent Jed in to inquire officially. Jed had local credentials to make inquiries. Wyatt waited patiently.

After a few minutes Jed came out, smiling. "The clerk remembered pointing out Mr. Howard to an older customer. He didn't realize the boarding house is owned by just Mrs. Howard."

"Did he know the older customer?"

"No, but he remembered his name. The customer said he wanted all mail for the Diamond House saved for him in his box. His name is Thomas Sherman."

"Now that's solid police work, son," Wyatt said. "What's the Diamond House?"

"Used to be a saloon and gambling house on the edge of town," Jed said. "Without drinking, it hasn't been making money. I think it's been closed all summer. It's not very big and looks run down."

"Let's go back and see if Kate knows this Thomas Sherman. If she does, we'll have a little chat with him. Sound good to you?"

"What if she doesn't know him?"

"We'll still talk to him," Wyatt said. "But let's hope she recognizes the name. Sounds like a problem from the past is back."

They retraced their steps to the hotel, and went through the lobby to the dress shop. Kate was sitting behind the counter with no customers.

"Tom Sherman?" she said. "Damn right I know him. I used to live with that ass until Doc came to town, and we fell in love. He runs sporting houses in working class towns, nothing fancy. He must want to set one up in my boarding house. I have ten rooms there, you know."

"Why would he send you that note?" Jed said. "Why not just come make you an offer? Besides, there are other places for sale in town."

"He's one nasty man. He tried making threats when I said I was leaving him, but Doc ran him out of town. I know he killed at least one man in a fight, so he's dangerous. Doc was more dangerous though, so Tom ran away."

"He might have calmed down a bit," Jed said. "He's kind of old."

"He wrote that note," Wyatt said. "We have to assume he means business. Let's go pay him a visit and find out for certain. It's time to wrap up this case."

He started for the door, then turned back. "Good luck with your new life here, Kate. If anyone else causes you a problem, Jed here can help you."

"I'm sorry I accused you, Wyatt," she said. "Thank you for your help."

"Least I could do. Doc was always there for me."

He nodded and led Jed back to the lobby.

"Should we go find Mr. Sherman now?" Jed said.

"What would you advise?" Wyatt tugged his hat onto his head.

"Would it be wrong to let the chief know what we've found out?"

"No, it would be wise to keep him informed. So lead the way to the police station."

The station was three blocks away. They passed the assay office on the way, where Wyatt read the hours on the window to be certain he could pick up his report. They paused for a moment before going into the police station.

"You fill the chief in on our progress," Wyatt said. "But then leave me alone with him for a couple of minutes before we go interview Sherman."

"I will," Jed said, looking a bit confused.

"Son, you've done a top-notch job today. I want to let your chief know that, and it might be awkward if you were standing there."

"Oh," Jed said. "I understand. Thank you."

He smiled broadly and led the way into the station.

There was an officer at a desk as they entered, who nodded at Jed as they went back to the chief's office at the rear of the building. There, they sat in front of Chief Steele's desk while Jed reviewed the day's findings.

"I had no idea Mrs. Howard was Big Nose Kate," Steele said. "I've heard stories about her and Doc Holliday. She was pretty wild in her younger days. Is her nose really that big?"

"She could outdrink and out-curse most men," Wyatt said, "but her nose is very normal. I called her that because she would stick her nose in everything. And she was damn smart, too. I'm happy she seems to have settled down with a good husband."

"What now, Officer Davis?" The chief looked at Jed, who stood up.

"We're going to go over and interview Mr. Sherman. If he's our man, I'll arrest him."

"Do you want anyone to back you up?"

"I think we're fine," Jed said. He saw Wyatt nod to him and turned to leave. "I'll be outside," he added.

"Jed Davis has done an excellent job today," Wyatt said. "I think you have a fine young man on your force."

"He's energetic and honest," Steele said. "But he's very young."

Wyatt nodded. "And innocent. When we get to Sherman's saloon, I'm leaving Jed outside. The sight of a uniform might spook Sherman, and I won't risk Jed being hurt. So if you have an officer who could be in the area, a little support would be welcome."

"Done," Steele said. He stood and reached across the desk to shake Wyatt's hand. "Thank you for working with Jed today, sir. It's been an honor meeting you."

Wyatt met Jed, who was checking his pistol, outside the chief's office. "All loaded now," Jed said. "I only have five bullets, like Brant told me." He nodded at the officer sitting at the desk.

"Brant is right," Wyatt said. "Carrying a round next to the firing pin is plumb dangerous if you fall or drop your pistol. You can kill yourself very quickly if your gun goes off accidentally. Besides, if you can't stop him with five bullets, one more probably won't do the trick."

They started back through town. Wyatt steered them to the assay office, where he picked up his report, paid the clerk, and pocketed his ore sample while Jed waited outside.

"I'm forcing us to take our time," Wyatt said. "It's never wise to rush into trouble. Take your time and you're ready when you find the situation."

Jed slowed down the pace a bit, until they reached The Diamond House, a shabby establishment that looked empty. "What now?" he said.

"If Sherman sees your uniform, he might panic," Wyatt said. "That would make him dangerous. So I'll go in and talk with him alone. If he says he's guilty, I'll bring him out and you can arrest him. You should stand ten feet from the door. If he tries to escape, hold him at gunpoint when he comes out. He's about my age, so he won't be too fast."

"Yes sir," Jed said, drawing his pistol.

"Safety off," Wyatt said, waiting while Jed checked and nodded. He held his gun with both hands, even though it shook with his nervousness.

Wyatt kept his hat on, opened the door, and stepped into the room. It was dusty, lit by two electric bulbs on the ceiling, Two tables near the front of the room were empty. In the back, an older man sat alone at a smaller table next to a rear door. He was playing solitaire.

Wyatt walked slowly toward him.

"Care for a game of cards?" The man wore a soiled white shirt with a faded suit coat over it. He was clean shaven with white hair.

"Are you Tom Sherman?" Wyatt said, stopping four feet from the table. He stopped and stood with his legs a bit spread.

"Depends," the man said. "Do I owe you money?"

"You wrote my friend Kate a threatening note."

"She's a whore and I'm taking over her boarding house. I'm Tom Sherman, and who the hell are you?"

"I'm Wyatt Earp."

"Heard you used to be the fastest gun in the west," Sherman said. "That true?"

"Bill Hickok was faster and deadlier. Do you seriously intend to burn her boarding house?"

"Wouldn't be smart. I want that house. If I burn it we all lose."

"Kate's not leaving."

"I'm afraid she's going to have an accident," Sherman said. "An old acquaintance is going to visit her and poor Kate will tragically die."

"How?" Wyatt said, stepping closer to the table.

"You're going to shoot her," Sherman said, "just after she signs the house over to me." Then you both will be out of my way." He grinned at Wyatt with bad teeth.

"Not likely. The police are just outside, and they know I don't carry a gun. Gave that up."

"But I do," Sherman said, standing up. He opened his coat to show Wyatt a small pistol in a black holster on his belt. "After you shoot Kate, I'll grab for the gun and it will go off, killing you. Then I'll be known as the man who shot Wyatt Earp."

"Remember who shot Bill Hickok?" Wyatt said. Sherman shook his head. "No one remembers cheap killers. And don't rely on that little pistol. It might not be enough to stop Kate or me."

"This way," Sherman said. "We're going out the back door and turning left. Kate's house is back behind us. Don't try running or calling out, or other people will get hurt. This is my last chance, and I mean business."

He opened the door, which swung out and to the right.

"I never ran before, and now I'm too old."

He shoved his hands into his jacket pockets as Sherman pushed him out the door, then followed. He grabbed the door to pull it shut, revealing Chief Steele, pistol drawn, standing next to the wall.

"Don't," Steele said, seeing Sherman's hand drop.

"Bonanza," Wyatt said. His hand came out of his jacket holding the small ore sack, which he swung backhand into Sherman's head. It made a satisfying crunch as it connected.

The man lurched sideways and his hand was on his pistol, still in its holster, so he was unable to catch himself. He hit the door and fell awkwardly onto the ground.

Steele reached down, pulled the small pistol out of the holster and stood up. "Now, Jed," he called, and the young officer stepped out from the side of the building. "Take this man to jail, Officer Davis."

He stood back while Jed pulled Sherman to his feet.

"Go along, Brant," called the chief, and another policeman stepped out from the other side of the building. "This is Jed's arrest, so kindly help him with the paperwork."

Brant nodded and took one of Sherman's arms. The two officers led Sherman away, dusty but unhurt.

"I appreciate you being behind that door," Wyatt said. "Haven't ever been shot, but I'd just as soon not try it now."

"Glad to help. And that ore bag to his head probably saved him from being shot."

"I'm glad it helped. The assay report says it won't be making me a tycoon."

"Well, sir, the least I can do is invite you to dinner this evening. My wife makes a tasty meatloaf. And I think I have a few bottles of confiscated beer I've kept cold. Please come." He smiled at Wyatt.

"I can't turn down a meal like that. Thank you."

"Do you mind kids?" Steele said. "I have two young sons."

"I enjoy youngsters. Never had any of my own, but thought it would have been a good thing."

An hour later Wyatt and Chief Steele were sitting behind the chief's house, enjoying a cold beer.

"What now?" Steele asked. "Any more travels planned?"

"None. I'm ready to get home to Josie, sit on my front porch, and listen to the train come through. I think I'm getting too old for these adventures."

Michael, Steele's ten year old, came to the door and announced dinner was ready. The men drained their beers, stood up, and went into the house.

"Meatloaf," Wyatt said, "Is my kind of adventure."

Since he had picked up his ore sample, Wyatt had no reason to stay for the noon train. He grabbed a breakfast of buckwheat cakes and coffee early and was on the train that left at 7:45. He reckoned he could be home shortly after noon, so leaned back in his seat and reviewed his stay in Prescott.

"Suppose I still carried a pistol," he thought. He might have shot Jed on his first evening in town. He probably would have shot Sherman, and that would have created all kinds of problems. The situation was resolved without shooting, which was good. He didn't regret giving up a sidearm.

At twenty minutes past noon, the train stopped briefly at Vidal. Wyatt stretched, pulled on his hat, and hurried to the door.

He climbed down, carrying his suitcase with the ore sack back in his pocket. It was a hot day, so he didn't hurry along the road to his house. He was looking forward to a cold glass of buttermilk.

But something was going on there. In front of his house was a large, familiar automobile. A man he didn't know was standing next to it, and moved to block the front walk as Wyatt approached.

"Sorry, sir, but you can't go in." The man had taken his jacket off, and Wyatt could easily see the revolver tucked in his belt.

"And just why is that?" Wyatt said, reaching into his pocket for the ore sample.

"My employer has said so," the man said. He looked beyond Wyatt, who turned and saw the sheriff's car coming quickly down the road. It skidded to a halt and Ray Gardner stepped out.

"Damnation," he said, staring. "It's you, Wyatt."

Wyatt heard the screen door squeak, and a tall man dressed as a cowhand stepped out. He pulled the screen door open.

"It can't be," he said. "Josie, come out here. Goodness gracious."

He smiled at Wyatt, holding the door for Josie, who came to the door with a handkerchief held to her face.

"Praise God," Josie said, hurrying down the walk and grabbing Wyatt. "You're home safe. Praise Jesus!"

"That's William S. Hart," Sheriff Gardner said to the driver.

"They said you were dead, Wyatt," Josie said, clutching his arm tightly. "They told me you were shot."

"I'm alive and not shot," Wyatt said. He reached out and shook Hart's hand. "What's going on, Bill?"

"Tom Mix called me from San Francisco and said the news was

on the wires. We thought reporters would show up here eventually, so I came down to be with Josie."

"I was at the other end of the county," Gardner said. "I stopped at a general store and news had come in by telegraph. I was hurrying here to check on Josie."

"I agreed with Tom that I would drive up to St George, Utah to identify you," Hart said. "We didn't want anyone asking Josie to do that."

"Thanks, Bill," Wyatt said. "I appreciate your kindness."

"I'm still driving up there. I want to see the poor devil who got killed and discover why they thought it was you."

"Can I hitch a ride?" Wyatt said. "I must admit I'm mighty curious." He looked at Josie. "But maybe I should stay here."

"No," she said. "You go right ahead. I need some time to settle myself down after all this. A quiet evening of prayer will do me wonders." She squeezed his arm. "But you come back to me, Wyatt"

"Carl will take your bag," Bill said.

"Sorry I didn't recognize you before, sir," Carl said, stowing Wyatt's valise in the automobile.

"You were doing your duty. I would never fault a man for that." He knew Carl had won a medal in the recent war.

He shook Carl's hand, then pulled out his ore sack and handed it to Josie. "We can discuss this when I get home, but it's neither good or bad."

"I'll get him home in a couple of days, Josie," Bill said. He held the door for Wyatt, who relaxed in the rear seat.

Bill shook Sheriff Gardner's hand, then climbed into the Packard's back seat with Wyatt. Carl pulled the car away from the house and drove down the dirt road toward the paved highway.

"This should take us about five hours," Bill said, "so we'll stop for some food along the way. I already arranged for three hotel rooms, thinking I would be bringing Josie, so we'll be comfortable this evening after the drive. I have my regular clothes with me; won't have to be dressed like a cowhand tomorrow."

Carl turned onto the paved road and accelerated, so there was a breeze cooling them. Both men settled back in the comfortable seating and dozed off and on for an hour or two. Carl was a good driver and the ride was smooth and relaxing.

When they were both awake, Wyatt yawned. "I just came home from two days in Arizona. Made me realize I've come to appreciate my rocking chair on the front porch."

"I'm getting close, Wyatt," Bill said. "I'm almost sixty, and the audiences won't believe I'm a young cowboy for much longer."

"You still look the part, Bill. That's what matters."

"For now, maybe. But in a few years those talking motion pictures you're waiting for will get here. And then I'm finished. I trained as a stage actor, Wyatt. I acted in Shakespeare productions in New York. I don't sound like a cowboy, and I never will. Winnie and I will sit by our swimming pool and drink fruit juice."

"That's right," Wyatt said. "I forgot you got married. Congratulations." He reached over and shook Bill's hand,

"This is my first trip away from her."

"Think you'll have kids?"

"I'd like to," Bill said. "Winnie is younger than I am."

The automobile slowed as Carl pulled into a parking strip next to a café.

"I'm leaving my hat and gun belt here," Bill said. "I wouldn't want to frighten anyone." Without his costume, Bill blended in nicely.

"I'll leave my hat as well," Wyatt said, smiling. "The sun shouldn't be too bright inside."

"I'll pull over to the gasoline pumps next door," Carl said. "We'll be ready to go after you gentlemen have your meals."

"Nonsense, Carl," Bill said. "Come in and join us. You need a break from driving. I insist."

~

There were only two tables of customers in the café, allowing Bill and Wyatt to sit in a booth near the back. Carl took a table a short distance away from theirs, keeping an eye on the waiters and customers.

"The studio hired Carl to be a bodyguard," Bill said. "He's very diligent. After that case with the murders last year, they're taking no chances."

"You never know about folks," Wyatt said. "Most people are honest and decent, but it's hard to tell sometimes."

"Before Carl got assigned to me, I bought two pistols that belonged to Billy the Kid. Used to be, I'd mount them and hang them at home. But after that killer was caught, I decided I'd keep them handy. So I cleaned them up, loaded them, and keep them hidden away in the Packard."

"That much firepower can hold off a whole band of desperadoes. I stopped carrying a pistol after that studio mess. But this jacket still has a special pocket if I ever change my mind."

Their food arrived, and they stopped talking and ate. Wyatt had the daily special, beef stew with a biscuit, while Bill had fried chicken. Carl had the chicken as well. They agreed it was a perfect lunch, washed down with chocolate milkshakes.

When they finished, and had washed up, Carl paid the bill, but Bill took a moment to sign autographs for the waiter and cook. Carl filled the gas tank, and then they were on the road again. As before, the drive was smooth and soothing.

Both men rested quietly or dozed until they pulled into St. George in the early evening.

Bill had booked them each a room at the Grand Utah Inn, an upscale hotel at the edge of the city. The entrance was a two-story patio with broad columns. He urged them to visit the restaurant if they were still hungry, but Wyatt was still full from earlier, and tired.

He did take advantage of the inn's laundry service. His suitcase had Prescott's dirty clothes, so he put those and what he was wearing in a laundry bag and hung it outside his door. He set the alarm clock in the room and climbed into the clean sheets, ready for sleep.

Wyatt slept soundly. After a refreshing shower, he put on his cleaned clothes and met Bill in the dining room. Carl had eaten earlier and was checking the automobile.

"I arranged to meet the police at the hospital morgue at nine," Bill said. "They may be expecting Josie as well. I anticipate newspaper reporters will be hovering for a story." Dressed in a white shirt and dark trousers, Bill looked nothing like the cowboy roles he was famous for playing.

"We might provide just that," Wyatt said. "Not every dead man attends his own news conference."

He ordered sausage and eggs with fried potatoes, while Bill chose hot waffles with fresh fruit. Although the city was heavily Mormon, the hotel served coffee to its guests. The food came promptly and was delicious. Wyatt realized how much he valued morning coffee.

After seconds on coffee, they met Carl outside and climbed into the automobile. Carl had gotten directions, so in ten minutes they arrived at the hospital's back entrance. The newsmen and the curious were upstairs and in the front so their arrival was not observed.

A police officer was waiting inside for Bill. "I'm sorry you travelled all this way," he said. "Mrs. Earp identified the body and gave us a description of the killer. We have a news conference set up for nine-thirty in the front lobby."

Bill looked at Wyatt, who raised his eyebrows. They were both interested to meet Mrs. Earp.

"We'd still like to see the body, since we were sent by the studio," Bill said. "Then we'll be happy to sit in on your news conference."

The police officer escorted them to the morgue, where a doctor met them. The officer told them how to find the news conference, then left them.

"Not a very warming spot," Wyatt said.

The doctor went to get the body, leaving them alone in the hot, dry facility.

"I wonder what Mrs. Earp looks like," said Wyatt. "I hope I married a beauty." He chuckled as the doctor wheeled a gurney into the room.

"This won't be gruesome," the doctor said. "I'll show you the victim's face only. He was shot twice in the chest."

"Thank you," Bill said, stepping up next to the sheet-covered gurney. He watched the doctor peel back the sheet, exposing an elderly man with a white handlebar moustache.

"Oh Hell," Wyatt said. "That's Charlie Hocksie. He ran a saloon with us in Nome, Alaska, years ago. He took off one day, and we never heard from him again."

"Then this isn't Wyatt Earp?" the doctor said, looking closely at the man's face. Both Wyatt and Hocksie wore moustaches, but the similarities ended there.

"Not yet," Bill said. "We'll go tell the police the man's real name."

"Thank you," Wyatt said, pulling his hat on as they walked out of the morgue.

"Now I'm curious," Bill said, as they walked down a corridor to the front lobby. "Why did someone shoot this Charlie fellow?"

When they reached the lobby, the police officer escorted Bill to the front of the room, while Wyatt stepped to the rear, behind the six newspaper reporters and photographers.

A police officer they hadn't met stepped forward and introduced himself as the chief. He explained that they were investigating a shooting and had asked the widow Earp to explain what had happened. "We could use as much publicity as possible on this," he said.

The widow stepped forward. Wyatt looked down a bit, shielding his face with his wide hat brim.

"Two days ago we were in our sandwich cafe," she said. "We had just finished with our lunch business and were cleaning up, when this man opened the door and told Wyatt he needed to see him outdoors."

"Did Mr. Earp agree?" the chief asked.

"Oh yes," she said. "People stop by most every day to meet him or get an autograph. So he stepped out, and I went back to the kitchen to put out the light. The next thing I knew I heard shouting and then two gunshots. I hurried out the door and there was poor Wyatt on the street, bleeding. And that man was pulling Wyatt's gun belt off him. Then he ran off when a couple of visitors ran up to help, but it was too late."

"So your husband didn't even draw his gun?" the chief asked.

"No, he never even loaded it," she said. "The tourists liked seeing it, since it was well-known."

"We're looking for a killer who shot down Mr. Earp in cold blood," the chief said. "Could you describe the pistol for the newspaper reporters?"

"It's bigger than a normal pistol," she said.

"What's bigger?" a reporter said. "What calibre is it?"

"I don't have the foggiest," she said. "The handle is carved up, I know. That's about all I remember."

"That isn't much to go on," the reporter said.

"The gun is a .45 calibre, single action Colt with a 12-inch barrel," Wyatt said, removing his hat. "The handle has the name Ned carved into it. The gun was a gift from Ned Buntline."

"Oh, God," the woman said, blushing and taking a step back. "I'm so sorry."

"Who is this man?" the chief said, looking at her. She shook her head, holding her hand to her mouth. She backed away from the front, shaking her head,

Bill stepped forward. "Chief, allow me to introduce my friend, the real Wyatt Earp."

Reporters turned and flashbulbs popped, while the chief had an officer lead the widow out of the lobby.

Wyatt stayed and warned reporters that there was still a murderer afoot. He stressed that the killer had shot a man he thought was Wyatt Earp, and that it was still cold-blooded murder. He then explained to the chief who the victim was and that the widow's name was Ayla Hocksie. It turned out that she and her husband had opened their lunch cafe several years earlier and had been moderately successful.

"What about the gun?" Bill said. "How did Charlie get his hands on it?"

"I actually gave it to him in Nome," Wyatt said. "It was awkward to wear in a holster, with that barrel. I know Bat Masterson got one, too, and he never wore it around either."

By the time all questions were answered, it was mid-afternoon. Telegrams had been sent by out-of-town reporters, and Wyatt was again alive and well.

Carl swung into the parking lot and picked them up

"What now?" Bill said. "We could get you home by a little after nine."

"And you'd be on the road until the wee hours," Wyatt said. "Let's stay here until morning and get a fresh start. Besides, leaving town now will feel like running away."

Carl drove them back to their inn, where he dropped them and went to park the automobile.

"I don't think this is over," Wyatt said. "If this shooter comes back, I'd rather have him find me here. I don't want Josie bothered."

"You think he's still around town?" Bill said.

"If not, he's heard the news and is either coming back or heading for the hills. I expect we'll know the difference by tonight. That's why I told the newspaper reporters we were staying here."

"I want to alert Carl," Bill said. "He'll be able to handle it if anything happens. But you ought to have a pistol, too, just in case."

"Having a gun didn't help Charlie. But if it makes you rest easier, Bill, I'll carry one in my jacket."

"It will ease my mind. Let's walk out to the Packard."

They strolled out to the parking area, where Carl had left the car. Bill opened the trunk, reached in and pulled out a wooden gun case. He opened it, and Wyatt saw a revolver with a polished wooden handle, obviously cleaned and well cared for.

"It's Billy the Kid's .44 calibre Colt," Bill said. "It's single action, but I have his .41 calibre double action, too, if you'd prefer."

"This should make a big bang," Wyatt said, smiling. "Maybe you should carry 'The Thunderer.'" He took the pistol from Bill, checked to see if it was loaded, and slid it into the pocket in his jacket.

"You know your guns, Wyatt," Bill said. "I'm impressed."

"These are from my younger days. Billy was killed while my brothers and I were in Tombstone."

"I believe I'll leave the other pistol here," Bill said. "If you and Carl can't stop this fellow, my chances would be altogether slim." He carefully put the pistol into the case and laid it down.

He closed the trunk, and they strolled back to the front door of the inn.

As they approached the entrance, a man stepped out from behind a pillar. He looked to be in his twenties, dressed in dirty pants and a blue shirt, and unshaven. He was wearing a gun belt with the

Buntline pistol in a holster.

"Which of you is Wyatt Earp?" he said, his voice loud. He hitched up his holster and glared at them.

"Why should it matter?" Bill said.

"Because I'm here to kill Wyatt Earp."

"Give it up, son," Wyatt said "You already killed an innocent man. It's time to stop." He turned to face the young man directly.

"So I got nothing to lose. I'll kill both of you if you don't say."

"Move away, Bill," Wyatt said. "This won't take long."

As Bill stepped off to the side, Wyatt opened his jacket. "That gun used to be unloaded," he said. "It wouldn't be fair to shoot you if you couldn't shoot back."

"It's loaded, old man," he said. His hand hovered over the pistol.

"It's a single action," Wyatt said. "You have to cock it before you can shoot it. If you wait to cock it until you've drawn it, I will have shot you dead already."

The man glanced down at the pistol, and lowered his hand.

"Now," said Wyatt. He smiled at the young man's fury,

He slipped the pistol out of his jacket and waited. The young man quickly cocked the Buntline and jerked it upwards. The front sight snagged on the bottom of the holster, causing his finger to pull against the trigger, firing the gun. He looked up at Wyatt.

"You got your foot," Wyatt said as the man let go of the pistol and staggered back. He stared as Wyatt slowly cocked his gun.

"No," the young man said. "I'm sorry."

"That you are," Wyatt said. He smiled at the wounded man and shook his head. Then he fired into the dirt, cocked the gun, and fired again. "Ought to get some attention."

Carl came through the inn door, gun drawn. Seeing Wyatt with the gun, he slid his into its holster and came forward to pin the man's arms behind him.

"That was quick," Wyatt said. "Thank you, Carl. I think this has solved our problem."

He handed his pistol to Bill, who had hurried forward. "Kinda thought this might happen," he said. "The reason Bat and I didn't carry this gun was that the front sight always snagged. Here's the secret." He reached down, took the pistol grip, shoved it into the holster, then twisted it away from the man's leg. He then lifted the pistol, and it slid out easily. "Took us years to figure it out."

Two police cars arrived then, and officers climbed out, guns drawn.

"All over, boys," Carl said. "Here's your killer. He managed to shoot himself in the foot trying to kill Mr. Earp."

The guns went away and the police surrounded the young man, handcuffed him, put him in one of the cars, and drove him to the hospital. Other officers wrote down statements from Wyatt, Bill, and Carl, finishing just as the chief arrived with a car of reporters.

The reporters took endless photographs, and then left for the hospital.

"Thank you, gentlemen," the chief said. He had been holding the Buntline during the photographs, but handed it to Wyatt. "This here is stolen property. I'm happy to return it to its rightful owner."

The chief and his officers climbed into their automobiles and departed, while Carl went into the inn to reserve a dinner table.

"Add this to your collection," Wyatt said. He handed the Buntline to Bill. "It's the same vintage as your other fine pistols."

They walked back to the Packard, and Bill put the guns securely in the trunk.

"Thank you, Wyatt. I shall cherish that gun."

"I'm glad. Just don't try any fast draw with it." He waited while Bill closed the Packard trunk.

"Dinner?" Bill said.

"An excellent idea."

Over steak, baked potatoes, and creamed spinach, the three men reviewed their day.

"If I may ask, sir," Carl said, "why didn't you shoot him? He deserved it."

"Thirty years ago I would have," Wyatt said. "The high society folks paid me and they liked it when I did. After Tombstone, the Earp name was tied to violence."

"But you represented the law," Bill said.

"All fine and good until there's trouble. Nowadays the police are plentiful. Still, young men like we saw today are looking to prove themselves through violence. They haven't been soldiers in war or ever been in a gunfight. They're play-acting like boys used to do with wooden pistols. But their guns are real. The world isn't about that anymore. Society has to figure it all out, but I'm too old to be involved."

"So what do you suggest, sir?" Carl said.

"Right now?" Wyatt smiled. "I suppose I'd be happy with a slice of apple pie with a hunk of cheddar cheese."

1938 – Hollywood, California

"Cut!" the director shouted. He looked up at the cameraman. "How was it, Hank?"

"Looks great, Mr. Ford."

"That's a wrap," the director said. He took off his cap and wiped his brow.

He looked up as a man dressed as Wyatt stood up from the table and came over, pulling off the thin, white moustache. "What do you think?" Ford asked.

"We did it," Tom Mix said. "No flashback to the OK Corral, just like Wyatt would have wanted. He would have loved it."

"Big adventures for those old guys."

"Ever notice that old pistol I have mounted in my office, next to the picture of Tony?" Tom asked. "That's the one. It's Wyatt's old gun."

"Did he ever tell Josie the whole story?"

"I don't know. He never mentioned it again to me. I guess we'll find out when she sees the movie."

"People call you the King of the Cowboys," Ford said. "But in a real sense, he was the king. We play with their stories. He lived them."

"Of course he was the king," Tom said. "Wyatt was the original."

The End
by Floyd "Nipper" Eisenhower

Nodding put down the novel and turned on his laptop email.

> Hey Nipper,
> I just finished 'Wyatt Retired' and loved it. I can only imagine how much work went into researching and writing it. I'd love to drop into the shop sometime soon and chat about Wyatt. Again, thanks for letting me read it!
> Dave

The next day he received a reply from Nipper:

> Greetings, Dave.
> I'm flattered by your kind comments. I enjoyed writing about Wyatt Earp. Many of the characters were real, but I confess I took liberties with the plot. Anyway, the shop has been quiet lately, so I got inspired to create a story with a character I created. See what you think!
>
> Mrs. Saks is arriving in two days with a moving van, so I'll have a neighbour. Looking forward to seeing you, Dave.
>
> Nipper

The Chestnut Kid and the Mail Order Bride

by Floyd "Nipper" Eisenhower

Emma Clark wiped the last breakfast dish and put down her towel. She shook her long brown hair, took off her new apron, and hung it from the hook David had put up for her. He had planned so carefully for her arrival a week ago and had been so thoughtful. With these mail-order marriages, you never knew. But Emma had hit a winner.

It hardly seemed possible they had been married only six days. Already she was learning where everything was in the general store in front of their living quarters. What a change from the dismal past.

A month ago she had been living in North Carolina, with little money and few choices since her mother's death. Zeb Church had wanted to marry her, but he was a thief, and she decided to escape the town. In Asheville she had seen a poster seeking mail-order brides for the Utah frontier and, with four dollars left in her purse, Emma had signed on.

Interrupting her reverie, David called, "Customers."

Shoppers didn't always stop by this early. It was time to get busy!

Emma smoothed her dress over her slim form and hurried out to join him. Outside the store, two men were dismounting and tying their horses. They were dressed in dirty clothes and both had dark beards.

Emma thought they were in their twenties, and both wore pistols, as most men in the area did. As they came in the open door, she stepped back behind David.

"Good morning, gents," David said. "What can I get for you?"

"Here's our list," one of the men said. He handed David a sheet of paper.

"Food and bullets," the other man said, glancing at Emma. He smiled. "You a hired girl?"

"Emma's my wife," David said, smiling at her.

She glanced at the list and started piling the food needed on the counter. David pulled out several boxes of ammunition and put them on the counter as well.

"That's the last of it," Emma said, putting down a bag of coffee. David started adding up the bill as the men glanced at each other.

"You happen to have a horse for sale?" The taller of the men stepped to the counter. He was looking over the shelves carefully.

"No, I don't," David said. "Just have one out back, but we need her for our wagon."

"Afraid we need it," the shorter man said. "Gotta have a horse for your wife to ride." He leered at Emma. "We're heading up into the high country. It's too far to make her walk."

"That's enough," David said. "People around here don't cotton to such talk. I have to ask you to pay up and to leave, pronto."

"We do talk rude," the taller man said. "We act rude, too. And we need your wife." He nodded at Emma. "Are you ready to leave?"

"Get out," Emma said. She backed up a step. She saw David reaching under the counter to bring his pistol up.

"Don't be stupid," the shorter man said. "There are two of us. One of us will shoot you and then take your wife and horse. There's an easier way."

"What?" David said, aiming the gun at him.

"This," the taller man said. David glanced at him as the man raised his pistol and fired once, hitting David in the chest.

"No!" Emma cried as her husband fell. But the shorter man reached out and grabbed her arm. He roughly pulled her away from David's body.

"You'll like Capitol Reef," he said. "Lots of privacy there. Now let's go get your horse."

He nodded to his partner and pulled Emma across the room. He yanked her to the door, as the taller man grabbed the food and bullets, put them in a grain sack, and then followed them out the door.

~

The next morning a man trotted his white horse along a trail near Sand Creek. It was an isolated spot, but he was familiar with the area and turned up a path towards a log house in a pine grove. He smelled wood smoke as he neared the house and dismounted.

He tied his horse to a rail outside the house, but waited beside it until the front door opened and a man stepped out. He was tall, over six feet, solidly built, clean-shaven with grey-flecked brown hair.

"Hey, Ridge," he said. "Come on up. I just brewed some coffee."

The rider climbed up the steps and shook hands. He took off his hat and smiled. "It's good to see you, Lurt."

They went inside and settled in front of the fireplace.

"What brings you out of town?" Lurt asked, blowing on his coffee to cool it down. "I don't normally see anyone unless I ride in. Is the saddle business slowing down?"

"Not at all," Ridge said. "But I gotta be honest, Lurt. There's a problem and we need your help." He saw his friend smile and felt a surge of guilt. Most local residents steered clear of the renowned gunfighter until they needed his help.

He put down his coffee mug. "Brent got a wire last night from the marshal. Yesterday two strangers up in Teasdale stopped in David Clark's store."

"Dave just got a new bride, I hear."

"That's the problem," Ridge said, shaking his head. "These outlaws shot and robbed David. The worst part is they took his wife with them."

"They took a woman?" Lurt stood up. "That just isn't tolerated in these parts. They'll be hunted down fast."

"The marshal is up near Salt Lake. He can't get there fast enough, and he doesn't think he could catch them." Ridge stood up. "He telegraphed and asked if you would try. You know Capitol Reef, and the men there will let you in."

"The outlaws," Lurt said. "But, how do you know they're headed that way? They could have gone three other directions."

"David lived long enough to write 'reef' in his blood on the floor. A posse tried to follow, but the ride got too rough for guys who don't know the area."

"Damn," Lurt said. "David was a good man. I'll ride out as soon as I can. Wire the marshal that I'm happy to help."

"Thanks, Lurt. Those outlaws will not be happy when the Chestnut Kid catches up with them." Ridge picked up his hat. "Want some company?"

"You know, Ridge, I think you should stay in town. If those two should change direction, you can handle them. Besides, you have a wife and kids. Keep them safe, okay?"

"Will do," Ridge said. "Come for dinner soon, will you? The boys miss seeing you."

They shook hands, and he took his leave.

Mounting up, he turned and started toward town at a canter. Two men would be no match for the kid. Besides, the kid knew the wild reef and the outlaws who lived there.

He smiled. Lurt had earned his name at seventeen, when he had ridden into the woods to practice shooting the old Colt his grandfather had left him. Coming home, he had heard shots from his family's property and spurred his horse to a gallop. He reached into his saddlebag and pulled out the old pistol, glad he had cleaned and reloaded it.

Coming into the clearing, Lurt saw his father lying in front of the house. One stranger stood on the porch, and four others sat on horses near his father's body. Without hesitating, Lurt galloped at the house, firing his first shot at the man on the porch.

As the man fell, Lurt swung the pistol to his right, and in two shots knocked two men from their saddles. He turned his horse to the left, straight at the last riders. Their horses backed sharply, slowing their riders in their draws. They had worn masks, which told Lurt they were invaders.

Lurt did not hesitate, shooting each of the men with his last bullets. Lurt had gotten home to save his mother and sister, and the young gunman's reputation was born. The teenage fast draw became a legend in Colorado.

Ridge shook his head as he rode back towards town. Not everyone realized who the quiet man in the woods was, but the two kidnappers would soon find out.

~

Lurt Chestnut watched Ridge ride away, then rinsed the coffee mugs in a bucket of clean well water. "Time to get back in the saddle," he said aloud. He loved the rugged land he would be riding into, but he knew he'd miss the warmth and safety of his cabin.

He went to a small closet and took out his handgun and holster. He made certain it was cleaned, oiled, and loaded. Unlike some gunfighters, he didn't wear a second pistol. One was enough.

~

The ride was hot and dusty. Emma's reins were tied to the horse in front of her, keeping her from riding away. She kept her head down, not wanting to look at the men who had taken her. She had no hat to keep her from being sunburned, and dust was covering her face and hands. She felt like sobbing, but she would never let these men see any weakness. She had come this far with her dignity intact, and she wasn't about to weaken now.

She had been living at home with her parents, working in their small store. It was why she'd answered the ad for a wife from the newspaper. Her father was sickly and had warned her that, without her mother, he'd be giving up the store soon.

This was the chance to start fresh, she had thought. She was twenty-two years old, almost a spinster, with no romantic prospects in her area. So she had answered the ad and two months later was on her way to Utah by train and then stagecoach.

"Takin' a break," the man in front said to her.

They stopped by a stream and dismounted. Emma slid off her horse quickly so neither of the men would touch her. She was going to be strong and fight any moves on their part.

The horses drank from the stream while the men chewed on some jerky. They offered Emma some, but she shook her head.

"Why did you make me come with you?" She looked at each man, not liking how they stared back.

"You're going to be our wife," the taller man said. "You'll cook and keep our cabin clean." He spat gristle out the side of his mouth. "I heard you called Emma back to the store. I'm Lucas. This here's Mark. He's my brother."

"Where are we going?" Emma looked from one to the other, and when Lucas answered, she realized he was the leader.

"We got a cabin up in the hills. Lawmen don't bother us up there, so don't be thinking about running away."

"No one will disturb us or hear you if you scream," Mark said. He leered at her.

Emma shivered at the way he looked at her body.

"Got a few more hours," Luke said. "Let's get going."

Emma patted the horse and softly stroked it. Like her, it was a prisoner. "I'm not a very good cook."

"You'll learn," Mark said. "Cooking ain't as important as keeping us happy." He smiled, and Emma noticed he was missing several teeth. If any opportunities came her way, she would escape.

Appearing in control of herself, she climbed onto her horse, not letting the men see her tears as they rode.

~

Lurt rode quickly, stopping only to water and to rest his horse. He fed it some grain from his saddlebag, then mounted and was moving again. So far the tracks were easy to follow. The men didn't think they'd be followed.

He had thought about where they would have entered the reef, and he took an old trail that would save him several hours. He watched the trail carefully, noticing fresh tracks as he approached a large boulder. He pulled up, waiting, until a man on a horse moved out onto the trail. He was holding a rifle, but lowered it and smiled when he saw Lurt.

"Look who's here," he said. "You're not on the run, are you, Kid?"

Lurt was known and welcome here. If the killers had come this way, they would have been stopped.

"Not any more," Lurt said, taking off his hat. "How are you, Butch?"

"Can't complain," the man said. "As long as folks leave us alone up here."

"They will. The marshal came up with all kinds of reasons to send me up here instead of coming himself."

"After the gang?"

"I wouldn't have come for that. I'm after two strangers. They stole a woman after shooting her husband."

"They brought her up here?" Butch asked. "What's the world coming to? No one messes with women."

"That's how I know they're strangers. Any man in his right mind would know you and your gang wouldn't put up with such non-sense."

"How can we help you, Lurt?"

"Just watch for them, in case I miss them. I think I can handle two."

"No doubt about that," Butch said. "Good luck to you."

Butch returned to his post among the boulders. Lurt started up again, knowing he had to hurry if the woman would have any hope of rescue.

An hour later, he saw a small cabin ahead, just off the trail. Two horses were tied near it, and a scruffy man stood outside, holding a rifle.

"Lookin' for something?" The man shifted the rifle slightly to point at Lurt.

"Just passing through," Lurt said. "Heading up to see my friends." He knew everyone was aware of the outlaws in Capital Reef territory.

He saw the rifle lower as the man relaxed.

"My brother just rode up that way, too," he said. "We got us a wo-man here the boys will like." His smile widened. "You know, you could be the first for five dollars."

"What's she look like?" Lurt said, looking at the cabin.

"Get out here, girl," the man said. His voice was gruff and cruel.

A young woman came to the doorway. Lurt saw the terror in her eyes and glanced back at the man.

"She looks good for five dollars," he said.

Lurt was disgusted by the man's behaviour, but waited for the right time to act. With his hand on his pistol and his eyes on the man, he swung down from his horse and handed the man a five dollar coin.

"Take her into the back room," the man said. "I'll keep watch out here."

Lurt stepped into the cabin and to the back room, where Emma huddled against the far wall in terror.

"Lie down," Lurt whispered, moving to the side and away from the girl. He turned and faced the door as he heard the man's boots on the dirt floor.

"Time's up," the man said, coming through the door. He saw the girl on the floor, then saw Lurt facing him. His mouth opened in surprise, then closed as he raised the rifle.

Emma would remember what happened next for years. She saw the rifle come up and started to close her eyes, when the stranger moved in a blur. She saw his pistol suddenly stretch toward Lucas and heard it boom twice. Through the smoke, she saw Lucas flung back out of the room.

Then the gun was back in the holster, and the man offered her his hand.

"Are you Emma?" He helped her up, smiling. "My name is Lurt, and I'm here to take you out of these hills and back to town."

Emma collapsed against him, sobbing. "His brother will be coming back. He has a gun, too."

"He won't be back to bother you," said Lurt. "You get whatever you need together, I'll bring you some water to wash up, and I'll take care of him." He nodded at the body beyond the doorway.

"When you're ready, we'll get you back to civilization."

He brought a bucket of water from the front room for her, then left her alone.

Lurt emptied the man's pockets, keeping his five dollars but setting aside what the men had taken from Emma and her husband. He pulled the body onto the pile of blankets along one wall, covering it with one of the larger blankets. He took a lamp from the table and poured oil onto the blanket and along the base of the walls.

He escorted Emma to her horse, then stepped back to the door and flicked a match into the cabin. The flames roared and smoke poured out of the door.

As the flames crackled, he looked at Emma. "No one will come along to read over this man's body," he said, "and we don't have time to bury him."

He helped Emma onto her horse, then tied the other horse to his saddle. He mounted his horse and led the way away from the cabin, pausing only when they heard a volley of shots from the canyon above.

"It's friends," he said, seeing the fear in Emma's eyes. "No one is left to come after you."

"They said there were outlaws up there," she said.

"Even outlaws have honor," Lurt said. "Women and children are treasured on the frontier. And whoever tries to hurt or take them is below contempt. Life is hard enough here without men like that among us. And now there are two fewer to worry about."

He turned and led her down the trail.

"I have nothing to go back to," Emma said. "I don't ever want to see that store again."

"We're not going back there. We're going to find a fresh start for you, with friends and a new life, if you want it."

"I do. But I would like to know your name."

"Forgive me," he said, turning in his saddle and raising his hat.

"I'm Lurt Chestnut. I live in the woods down below."

"Thank you, Lurt Chestnut. It's an honor to meet you." She saw the pale forehead when he raised his hat, in contrast with his deeply tanned face; Lurt Chestnut was a real westerner.

"We'll stop and water the horses in a bit," he said, turning back to watch the trail ahead. "I believe we'll get to town just after dark."

"Are you from Utah, Lurt?" He seemed so at home on this trail.

"No ma'am. I was brought up in Colorado, up near Leadville. My family still lives there."

"Do you ever see them?"

"Not often, but they know where I am if they need me."

He didn't seem to want to explain, so they rode in silence for a bit.

"Think you'll head back east?" Lurt asked, without turning in his saddle.

She realized it was a choice she had to make, "No. This is where I want to be."

"The town we're headed to needs a store. Used to be one, but the owner got too old." He turned again. "It even has a place to live above the store. And this place is right in town. Lots of folks nearby."

"I don't have any money," Emma said. "That's a problem."

"But you will," Lurt said. "When your old store sells, you'll get that money. We could get the merchandise brought to town, since it's already yours. I got the cash they stole from you, too. Nice little family town."

They rode in silence for a bit. At the foot of the trail they stopped to water the horses and stretch. Lurt built a small fire and brewed some coffee. They took turns drinking from his one cup, then mounted up as the afternoon wore on.

"We should get there just about dinner time," he said. "My friends will have a hot supper and fresh bed for you."

"I think I'd be interested in that store," she said. "It sounds like a nice place to settle." She realized her future was once more hers to plan.

"It is. If I was to live in a town, it would be my choice."

"Where do you live, then?"

"Out in the woods," Lurt said. "I raise some horses and keep to myself." He smiled, knowing some folks would call him a hermit.

He turned in his saddle and looked at her. "When I'm in town too long, trouble comes along. So it's best if I'm out of sight." He saw her look of concern. "But I'll be a customer at your store." He smiled and swung back to face the trail.

At six-thirty, they rode into town. Townspeople were at home, but the saloon was open for business. They rode on down the street, and Lurt pointed out the empty store. It was bigger than David's, and Emma thought it seemed in fine shape.

Then they reached Ridge's house and dismounted. Ridge came outside and welcomed them, followed by his wife, Georgene, and their two young sons. Dinner was waiting, and Georgene ushered Emma into their home.

They offered to let Lurt spend the night, but he took the horses up the street to the livery stable and settled them in with grain and rubdowns. When he finished, it was dark, and he was too tired to eat, so he spread his blanket near his horse, settled onto the fresh hay, and fell asleep easily.

He awoke the next morning just after eight. He brushed the hay from his clothes and pumped a basin of fresh water to wash his face and hands. He packed his belongings in his bedroll, left it with his saddle, then set out to get some breakfast at the small cafe near the boarding house. It was down the main street, past the saloon, and on the way to Ridge's house.

As he walked past the saloon, Lurt saw a man move out from the saloon to the street.

"Hey," the man said, and then fired his pistol.

Lurt felt a sharp blow to his right hip and fell, turning his head as he hit the dusty street so he could see his attacker. A young man wearing a buckskin shirt turned and stepped back into the saloon without looking to see if Lurt had survived.

Lurt had, and he was mad. He lay still for a moment, then slid his hand down his side to inspect the wound. His hip throbbed, but he found no blood. Instead, he found a hole in his holster where the bullet had struck.

Slowly drawing his pistol, Lurt saw the cylinder was dented and jammed, so it wouldn't fire. He was lucky he rode with an empty chamber. It only gave him five shots, but in this case it had saved him from serious injury.

Hot anger flooded him as he realized how close he had come to being murdered. He knew the feeling; it was what he had felt as a young man, seeing his father lying in front of the house.

The anger pulled him to his feet, taking control, and he walked to the saloon, sliding the broken gun into the holster.

He pushed the door open and stepped in. The young man was at the bar, talking to the bartender. It was too early for any other customers. Even the elderly barflies stayed home until almost noon.

"I outdrew the fastest gun," the young man was saying.

"That only works when the other guy is looking at you," Lurt said, stepping forward. "Now I'm looking, so reach for your gun."

He walked slowly towards the bar, watching the young man closely. There was no cold hardness in his eyes, but fear. The bartender stepped away, reaching under the bar.

"This is your play," Lurt said. "Any last words?" He rested his hand near his pistol, staring at the young man, watching him muster his courage.

The moment came, and the young man grabbed for his pistol. But as his gun rose to the edge of the holster, he saw Lurt's pistol inches from his face. The muzzle looked huge.

The young man dropped his gun back into the holster and looked as though he might start crying.

"Where's your horse?" Lurt said.

"Tied just outside."

"You tried to kill me. I'll give you five minutes to get on your horse and ride. Don't come back to this town. If you do, I will shoot you."

The young man nodded. "Thank you," he said. "I won't come back. I'm sorry."

He hurried from the saloon and, within minutes, Lurt heard a horse galloping down the street.

"Your pistol don't look so good," the bartender said. "I got a spare you can use if you want."

"Thank you, but no," Lurt said. "I have another one back in my saddlebag." He was grateful he was always prepared.

"You were decent to that young fool. You're always welcome here." The bartender reached a hand across the bar. "I'm Chuck."

"Good to meet you, sir. I'm Lurt." As they shook hands, a thought came to Lurt. "Chuck, do you know why the old store is still closed?"

"Old man Richards won't sell to anyone he thinks is Mormon. He made a lot of money selling coffee and such to settlers, and he knows Mormons don't hanker for that. Not too logical, from my point of view. Mormons are moving in all around here, but folks still keep me busy."

"It takes all kinds" Lurt said. "Thanks, Chuck."

As he turned to leave, he was already thinking.

He went out the door and walked down to the cafe. After breakfast and hot coffee, he walked across the street to an attorney's office. The man had helped Lurt buy his ranch quietly and could be trusted. Lurt's plan was in place as he entered the office.

An hour later, he left the office and crossed over to the saddle shop. Ridge wasn't there yet, so Lurt walked further up the street to Ridge's house. Within minutes of knocking, he was standing in the parlour with a new mug of coffee. After his night on the hay, it was hot and energizing

He sat down with the coffee and relaxed.

Ridge, Georgene, and Emma watched him take his first swallow.

"I've had a busy morning, but I have an idea for Emma," he said, putting down the coffee cup. "Just to be sure I understand your thoughts, you'd rather be here in town and working in a general store, instead of going back east or working in David's store."

"I couldn't go back there," she said. "And I have to find work to survive here."

"I just had a thought," said Georgene. "The general store is empty here in town. I've heard it's for sale."

"It was," said Lurt. "But the owner got an offer from a non-Mormon this morning and accepted. The new owner will want someone with experience helping out, so I know you can work there as much as you want."

Ridge looked at him, smiling. "So who bought the store?"

"I did. But I know nothing about stores, so I need a partner." He looked at Emma. "Interested?"

"Gosh, of course I am," she said. "But you know I have no money to invest, or even to stock an empty store."

"By tomorrow the bank will have funds for you to use for whatever you need. Ridge will help find someone to move the goods from your old store down here. You can also bring your furniture for the second floor, where you can live. Until then, we can get you a room at the boarding house."

Emma was trying to hide her tears, but without much luck. "How can I pay you back? This will cost you a fortune."

"After the move, you can sell the store you had with David. Pay me what you get from the sale, and we'll have papers drawn up listing you as owning fifty-one percent of the store here, and its contents. Sound fair?"

"More than fair," she said.

"One more detail," Lurt said. "I'll come to town and help out when I can. Instead of you paying me, I'll accept a home-cooked meal for my services."

"Any time," Emma said.

"nd no more talk of the boarding house," Georgene said. "You stay with us until you have a bed and furniture in the store. That boarding house isn't as clean as a person would hope."

"Sounds good," Lurt said. "Now, I want to head for home and get cleaned up a mite. I'll try to get into town in a few days."

"May I give you a hug?" Emma said, as Lurt stood to leave. She stepped close and wrapped her arms around him. She had tears on her cheeks.

Ridge smiled to see Lurt blush.

"You saved my life and gave me a new one," she said. "I will never forget that."

Before Lurt could answer, someone knocked loudly at the door. They all turned at the urgency.

Ridge crossed the room and opened the door, finding an excited Brent, the local barber and Wells Fargo agent.

"Thank the Lord you're still here, Mr. Chestnut. This telegram just came in from Colorado for you. I saw your horse at the stable and hoped you'd be with Ridge."

He handed the telegram to Lurt, who opened it at once.

"Damn," he said, showing them the message:

LURT COME HOME. MA NEEDS YOU.

"From my sister," he said. "I'll stop at the cabin, get cleaned up, and ride out on a fresh horse. But I'll be back as soon as I can."

Emma joined Ridge at the door as Lurt headed down the street to the stable. "I hope everything works out," she said.

"With Lurt Chestnut coming to help, it will," Ridge said. "We're lucky to call him a friend."

Drive Thru Christmas

There wasn't anything special about the fat man's order; he always ate that much. What set that night apart was the fact it was Christmas Eve, and I, for one, didn't want to spend it selling doughnuts and coffee to people who didn't have any place better to be.

Madeline and her senior fitness class had eaten lunch and gone to church or home to family gatherings. Archie and the older gents had been in for early breakfast and had long since left to spend the day with their grandkids. But there I was, under the bright red sign shining away into the cloudy evening sky, just waiting for closing time.

I should have known I was in for a strange night when I took over for Brenda at the takeout window. She was on early break to call her husband. I didn't know what was going on, but they were having some kind of trouble. Anyway, I slipped on the headset and clipped the transmitter to my belt.

"Merry Christmas," I said. "May I take your order?"

"I'm stuck at the stoplight," a deep, syrupy voice said. I somehow knew she was blonde. "But I'm thinking about being with you in front of the fireplace."

"May I take your order?" I said. "Hello?" I felt like an idiot. I hated talking into that little microphone.

Her voice seemed to be growing fainter. I leaned forward and looked back to the ordering box. I wasn't surprised to see the drive was empty. Somehow I'd picked up a mobile telephone transmission. It happened to Brenda a lot.

"Merry Christmas," I called softly into the microphone, a farewell gesture. The holiday phantom was gone.

"Same to you," a husky male voice said.

I leaned forward and saw the pickup truck.

"And gimme two turkey sandwiches, two large fries, and two large coffees, black." I punched in the order and heard the pickup driver belch.

"Please pull forward to the window," I said.

I put the sandwich order in, got the fries, and poured the coffees. I took them to the window, got the man's money, and gave him change, just as his hot sandwiches were ready. Where was that blonde going?

"That was quick," the man said. "Thanks."

"Merry Christmas," I said again, watching him pull out. He was a pleasant guy after all.

Then Brenda was back, her eyes swollen and teary. "Thanks," she said.

"You okay?" I said, unclipping the radio that started it all.

"Oh yeah. It's just Angus. He lost his job at the radio station last week, and he's feeling pretty beat up by it all."

"Doesn't make for a great holiday. Any chance of a new job?"

"I can't get him to get out and look. He knew the station was losing money and all, but he feels like he did something wrong. He was maintenance, you know."

"Well," I said, going back to my normal spot on the counter, "he can always come here." I wasn't being serious when I blurted it out.

We laughed, but not too hard. Neither of us planned to make this a career. I'm only twenty-three, and selling doughnuts and coffee loses its thrill after a year or two.

But what choice do I have? My parents aren't rich, and I want to be a journalist, which usually requires a university degree. At least this job lets me work with decent people and stay warm. It could be a lot worse.

So I'm in school, taking one course at a time, and working my butt off. I drive to school in the mornings and do my homework, then come here at four. I dream of seeing my byline in the *Chronicle-Herald*, but until a good story comes along or I graduate, here I am.

"Let's get the cups refilled while it's quiet."

It had been too pleasant. Odetta, our manager, had been in the back, counting coffee cartons. Now she was here, a little deaf, shouting out instructions.

"I did that already, Odetta," I said. Dealing with her would be so much easier if she would look before firing off orders, but she followed the management handbook's schedule, whether it was needed or not.

"Let's look sharp, people," she barked. "This may be Christmas Eve, but we're still open for business."

She was about to say more, but the door opened and a customer came in. Odetta moved over to inspect the takeout area.

"May I help you?" I asked. A lobsterman, I thought. He was wearing jeans, two sweatshirts, and heavy rubber boots.

"Yeah. I'd like two hamburgers, large fries, and a large coffee, black. For here." He glanced behind me at the menu sign. "No cheese on those burgers."

"Right," I said, punching in his order. He handed me a twenty and I gave him his change. "No cheese."

"I hate that stuff," he said. "I always have hated it. Cheese."

"Right on." I got out a tray, put a placemat on it, and went for his coffee.

"I won't touch any of it," he said, putting away his wallet and shaking his head. "All those cow products are poison to your system. Cheese, milk, eggs. I'm strictly meat and potatoes."

"That's smart," I said, putting his burgers on the tray.

"Even yogourt." He picked up his tray. "They won't tell you, but it has milk in it, too. It's printed right there on the label. It's poison, just like all those cow products."

I knew Chuck and Rick, who were cooking, would love this conversation, and I almost had a chance to go back and to tell them about it. But just as the lobsterman reached a table and put his tray down, a woman came through the door.

She stood just inside, looking around for someone. She was maybe fifty, wearing slacks and a parka, with graying blonde hair. But what stood out were her split lip and her right eye, which was nearly swollen shut.

I guess she didn't see anyone she knew. So she turned and took a seat at the table closest to the door.

"Odetta," I said, going over to the takeout window. "That lady's hurt. Maybe we should get her some help. Either she was in a crash or someone hit her."

"What do I do?" Odetta whispered. "Should I talk to her?" This wasn't in her manager's guide, I guessed.

Just then an older woman walked in wearing a suit and longer overcoat. She spied the blonde woman at once and went straight to her. She put her hand on the woman's shoulder, spoke to her quietly, then came over to the counter.

"May I help you?" I said.

"Yes. Two large double doubles and a cup of ice, please. The lady over there has a split lip."

"No problem," I said, pouring the coffee. "Is she okay?"

"Her face hurts," the woman said as she gave me money. "Her husband beat her up this afternoon, and she finally got up the nerve to walk out. So I'm taking her over to the Haven Sanctuary at the hospital. We're a new shelter for abused women and children."

I gave her the ice in a plastic bag, and she went back to the table. She sat across from the injured woman and handed her the ice. They sipped their coffee.

"Christmas Eve and he beat her up," Odetta said quietly. "That just isn't right."

The door opened, and the fat man came in with his nephew. They were becoming regulars, stopping in for dinner every week or so. The fat man was old, and weighed close to three hundred. My dad is big at two sixty, but this man was just plain huge.

He walked slowly, with a cane, and his nephew had to help him into a booth. Then the nephew, a wiry man of about forty, came over to order.

"Two double cheeseburgers, two large fries, and a chocolate shake, for here," he said.

"Anything else, sir?" I asked.

"Yes. For myself I'd like a chicken sandwich and a small black coffee."

It was no surprise; the old man ate that way every time they came in. His size was no mystery to us. We knew his habits.

I got the food together and gave it to the nephew.

"That just isn't a healthy meal," Odetta said. "All those fries."

"He isn't going to die young," I said.

I hadn't seen him come in, but suddenly I realized I was being watched. A tall, muscular man in a wool parka stood just inside the door, looking around. He was clearly upset, and then I remembered the woman with the split lip.

"Uh-oh," I said.

Odetta had already reached for her phone when the man looked at us and smiled. I'd met him over the summer at the company barbecue. Someone's husband.

"Angus," Brenda said, coming past us. "Be right back."

She hurried over to him, gave him a hug, and steered him to an empty booth. They sat together, chatting softly.

"Is it snowing yet?" Chuck called from the back.

"Not yet," Odetta said. "You have the grille cleaned yet?"

She headed back to keep the troops in line while I wiped the counter for about the tenth time that hour.

"Excuse me." The nephew was at the register. "Can someone help me? Uncle Chris can't get out of the booth."

"Odetta," I called as I went around the counter.

He was wedged tight. He'd gone through both burgers and most of the fries, and that had done the trick. Uncle Chris was a prisoner in the booth.

The problem was that, besides his bulk, Uncle Chris was about eighty. His arms were frail and brittle, so we didn't dare pull too hard. Even his hands felt fragile.

"I have to go," he said.

"We'll get you out," I said, looking under the table. We couldn't slide him out that way.

"No, I mean I have to go soon!" he said.

"What's that? Speak up a little," Odetta said.

He glared at her. "I'm stuck in the booth, and I have to go to the washroom."

"Should I call the fire department?" Odetta said. "Otherwise we may be here until tomorrow."

"Christmas?" Uncle Chris said. "I don't want to stay here all night. And I don't want to miss Christmas dinner with my family."

"No worries," the woman from the shelter said. "They'll have you out in no time flat."

Uncle Chris rolled his eyes. He wasn't convinced.

"Need a hand?" Angus was beside me, his dark eyes now concerned and gentle. He sat down on the edge of the bench beside Uncle Chris. "You live near here?"

"Part of the year," Uncle Chris said. "And I want to go home. I have to change." He tried to wiggle but it didn't work. He was wedged tight.

"I knew it."

Everyone turned to see the lobsterman standing on the bench at his booth, looking down at us.

"You ate cheese with those burgers. That poison will kill you dead."

"I'm not dying," Uncle Chris said. "I'm just stuck, and it's Christmas Eve." His voice was sounding desperate. He tried twisting again with no luck.

"Let's all calm down now," Odetta said.

"Hey dude, it's snowing."

I turned and saw Chuck and Rick at the counter, grinning.

"I have to get out of here," Uncle Chris said. "I'm Santa Claus." Everyone got quiet and stared at him.

"Whoa," Rick said. "And he came in here to eat."

"He means he's being Santa at the hospital tonight," his nephew said. "He's not the real Santa Claus."

"Ask them about cheese at the hospital," the lobsterman said. "They'll tell you it plugs your veins."

Everyone turned again to look at him. "Hey! What's in that cup?"

"It's a chocolate shake," the nephew said. I noticed he was wringing his hands.

"A milkshake?" The lobsterman jumped down and ran across the room. "That's what did it. Poison in a cup! Death with sugar in it."

"That's enough." Odetta waved her arms and everyone turned to look at her. "Don't you be blaming our shakes for this accident. We serve low fat in every shake."

"Low fat," Angus whispered to Uncle Chris. "That'll teach you to go on a diet at Christmas."

"Some diet," the fat man chuckled.

Then he began to laugh out loud. He leaned back and guffawed, just as Angus flexed hard, put his arm around the fat man's shoulders and pulled. I held my breath and watched.

The seat back groaned, and Uncle Chris came sliding out, supported by Angus.

"Thank you, young man," Uncle Chris said, shaking hands with Angus. "It looks like I get to be Santa tonight after all." He turned and hurried to the men's room.

Angus was waiting when he came out a few minutes later. "If you run across a job in that bag of yours tonight, you know where to find me," he said. He was smiling about the job now. It would be okay.

"I might be able to help," the woman from the centre said. "We need someone to be a driver and do a bit of maintenance."

"Now, wait," Odetta said. "I think we could come up with an offer here, too."

All of a sudden the Christmas Spirit was at work.

"My God," Angus said. "This is gonna be a good Christmas after all."

"I have to fly," Uncle Chris said. "I wish you all a very Happy Christmas."

He paused and looked at the lobsterman. "You're right to scold me," he said. "I ought to be eating tofu. It has no cow in it."

"You're okay, Santa," the lobsterman said. "Merry Christmas."

Uncle Chris nodded to his nephew, grabbed his cane, and started for the door. I jumped ahead and opened it for him, looking out at the snow.

"We're closing early, people," Odetta said. "It's Christmas Eve."

Uncle Chris winked at me as he passed and ventured into the snowy night. Then he turned and met my eyes. "Get typing, young man. See what you make of it all. I've done my part, you know."

The large red sign above us blinked off then, and I could see beyond the parking lot to strings of twinkling coloured lights decorating homes and stores just down the street. I heard laughter behind me in the restaurant and felt it flow out and surround me in a rush of warmth and dizziness.

"Goodnight," his voice called. "Merry Christmas."

And then the wind picked up a swirl of snow, and the holiday night was upon me.

Fat Nancy's Return

To Wayne Anderson at eighteen, snow was like the sea. In its quiet, sifting rhythm, he found a deep calm. On the surface was beauty which refreshed him deeply.

Yet just beneath that surface tranquility lurked the very source of earthly power, which man both fears and worships. To taunt the snow, to sail the sea, is to associate directly with that power, while at the same time conquering it by avoiding its final offering, death. The balance is always present, quietly waiting.

To recognize the relationship is awareness, and to enjoy it is to live life from the heart.

On New Year's Eve, it had been snowing for three hours when Wayne left his house to hike the three blocks to Eugene's. It would be a hard night for travel, but that would be the least of his concerns. Tonight he would reunite with his girlfriend, his woman.

Carol was here, or at least in town, staying up at the summer camp lodge for a holiday staff reunion. And tonight they would be together, although, at her parents' urging, they wouldn't be alone. Eugene and his steady girl, Virginia, were driving them up to a dance in Mabou. The Red Shoe was closed for the winter, but the firehouse social hall was bigger anyway.

"Now you boys be careful," Mrs. Jenkins said. "There's gonna be a lot of drunkards on them roads tonight. That's why we're staying put and watching a show."

She poured a splash of evaporated milk into her coffee from a small can and glanced over at her husband, who was sitting at the kitchen table, chewing beef stew.

"Take it real slow, Eugene," he said, looking up. He lifted the tab on a can of Keith's and poured it into his glass. "Real slow."

"Don't worry, I can drive," Eugene said, pulling on his coat. "Happy New Year, now. See you after midnight." He bent and kissed his mother's cheek.

He led the way out the back door and across the cold, grey porch, through the torn screen door, and into the snowy yard. "Parents," he said, opening his car door.

It felt good to be back in the battered white Chevy. The car reminded Wayne of their summers together, of countless evenings spent cruising, and of at least two dates with Carol last summer. He recalled the Inverness carnival, where Eugene had thrown up his french fries on the Ferris wheel. The other time, they'd gone roller skating in Cheticamp and shared a pizza with Virginia and Eugene. Both nights had ended with good-nights whispered in the parked car, long, sweaty, groping minutes before Carol made him stop and take her back to the lodge. He hadn't seen her all fall and had missed her.

Eugene had let him drive those times, but tonight he could relax with Carol and be driven.

The road was slippery. Eugene drove slowly, letting the snowflakes dodge up through the lights, over the windshield, then back into the night behind.

It took them nearly fifteen minutes to reach Virginia's farm, where Eugene pulled as closely to the house as he could, then stomped up to the house while Wayne sat back and waited.

Somehow the backseat of the old car flooded him with memories of Carol. The autumn telephone calls, emails, and brief visits after volleyball games had left her distant, a fragment, a figure no longer real. But here, where they had been together under the summer stars, the memory was alive.

"Hey, Wayne," Virginia said, sliding in past the steering wheel and smiling back at him. "Some night for a hoedown, ain't it?"

"Hope it's good," he said. No big band or rock tonight. There would be Celtic tunes and lots of country classics.

Eugene started the car, backed out, and they were on the way up the camp road. The gate was open, so Eugene pulled up the drive to the lodge, its lights lonely among the other dark, shuttered buildings. On summer nights the campus was lit and lively, but tonight it felt isolated and cold.

Wayne crawled out, hopping through the snow to the porch, smelling wood smoke in the cold night air. He stomped his feet on the stone floor of the porch, but before he could knock on the door it shook, then jerked open, and Carol stepped out. She was here, finally, after such a long time.

She pulled the door shut behind her, radiant in the summer's bug-yellow porch lights, and came into his arms. As golden and warm and beautiful as ever.

Together they hopped back to the Chevy, where he held the door for her. She slid over, making room, and he got in and pulled the door shut behind him.

After the usual greetings and laughs, Eugene turned the car around and headed down the mountain.

"Ever been to a barn dance before?" Virginia said. "Tonight will be more of a ceilidh, I guess."

"No," Carol said, squeezing Wayne's hand. "Is there a band?"

"A band?" Eugene said, turning down the country song playing on the CD. "Shoot. Fat Nancy's gonna be there."

When Carol said nothing, he went on. "Never heard of Fat Nancy? Shoot, she's got three CDs out and she's been on the country charts a couple of times up in Newfoundland, where she's from. Tonight's her first show in Mabou in over a year. She's great!"

He leaned forward to peer ahead into the snow. The road was slippery, so he drove with care, both hands clamped on the wheel.

The firehouse social hall was ideal for country concerts. At one end of the big hall stood clusters of folding tables, with folding chairs around them. Other chairs edged the polished wooden floor, set back against the yellow cinder block walls. In the middle of the hall, to one side, was a wooden platform with several stools and microphones on it. The makeshift stage was ready for the evening.

Over the platform, in the smoky light, was a banner announcing

FAT NANCY PEPPER AND THE GANDER GIRLS

but the band was nowhere in sight.

Wayne stood just inside the door with Carol and Virginia while Eugene parked in the freshly-plowed lot. When he came stomping in behind them, he was carrying a brown grocery bag. He handed it carefully to Wayne.

"They can't sell liquor in here," he said to Carol. "So they sell cups and ice and we bring our own booze. Dumb laws."

No one seemed too upset by the laws, as most occupied tables had one or more liquor bottles in plain sight.

Eugene walked over to the refreshment stand near the door, paid their admission and drink fees, and returned with four cups and a small bag of ice. He led them down the hall to the tables, choosing one near the edge of the building.

"I bet you could be five years old and drink in here tonight," Virginia said. "But finally we're legal for New Year's. We're grown ups tonight. Wow."

She watched Wayne pull a bottle of cheap vodka and two quarts of Collins mixer out of the paper bag. He mixed drinks in the cups Eugene had bought, then handed them out.

"If a man can't drink when he's living, he sure can't drink when he's dead," Eugene said, raising his red plastic cup. "So I say let's get some practice while we're living."

Wayne turned to Carol, beside him, and raised his cup. "To the warmth of last summer," he said.

"To the warmth ahead," she said.

As their cups touched, their hands did as well, lingering before they drank.

"Fat Nancy's really packing them in," Eugene said. "Just look at all them people." He rubbed at his ear, realized he looked foolish and grinned. "Shoot."

Wayne watched the couples coming in, taking off their coats, then wandering toward the empty tables. Most of the women were in their late twenties, he guessed, and looked like they were out for a big fling. They wore bright dresses or pants, while their husbands, who seemed mostly drunk already, wore tight white shirts and cowboy boots.

"Here we go," Eugene said, pointing to the band platform.

Four young women in pale blue cowboy shirts and jeans climbed onto the stage, twisting their microphone cables and adjusting their instruments.

As The Gander Girls took their places on the stage, the excitement was growing.

Finally one of them, the guitar player, leaned into a microphone and cleared her throat as the lights dimmed. "Folks, it gives me pleasure to introduce a little gal who most of you have heard since she was knee high to a duck. Let's all give a big Caper welcome to Miss Fat Nancy Pepper!"

She practically rolled onto the stage. There must have been three hundred pounds of Fat Nancy, all stuffed into a bright blue cowgirl suit with silver spangles. Her blonde, starchy hair was crammed into a white straw hat, held in place with a string looped under her fleshy chin. Her face was bloated and pink, but she smiled warmly as she pulled her microphone out of the stand.

"Thank y'all so much," she said. "We're gonna sing a bunch of our hits for you tonight and give you all a real whompin' New Year's, all right?" She held her hand behind her ear to encourage their response.

The crowd cheered loudly as Fat Nancy nodded to her band to begin. The song was loud, and the band was good.

Wayne hadn't heard the song before, but he listened carefully, impressed as always by Fat Nancy's voice. She sang with her eyes shut, enjoying the song, giving it her full attention. Her voice was husky but strong, and Wayne was glad to see Carol clapping loudly when the song ended.

"She's great," Carol shouted, while Eugene mixed more drinks for them. "How old is she?"

"She's gotta be in her late forties," Wayne said.

"She's older than my parents," Virginia said. "I'd say fifty, if not more."

Wayne looked at Carol, who met his eyes and smiled. Her cheeks were flushed from the drinks and excitement. The night was perfect so far.

When the band began a polka, he asked her to dance, and together they braved the highly waxed floor, laughing and happy.

The next few hours passed quickly. They drank, danced, and listened to Fat Nancy sing her favourite songs. She stood at the edge of the platform, rivulets of sweat dripping from her face, laughing and singing and taking frequent swallows from a flask herself.

Just before midnight, Nancy leaned into her microphone and cleared her throat. "Folks," she said. "We've got but time for one more song before the year checks out, and I want to dedicate it to Wayne and Carol."

Their eyes met as they stood and moved together.

The crowd applauded as Wayne caught sight of Eugene standing next to the platform, drunk and smiling. Then he walked carefully back to Virginia.

It was a slow song. Carol moved into his arms, and they danced together tightly in front of the band platform. When the song ended, they stayed there together, holding each other.

"Here it comes, folks," Fat Nancy said, looking at her watch. "Get ready, now." The year was ending and a new one was starting.

As the crowd quieted, Wayne kissed Carol's cheek and she smiled up at him.

"Ten," Fat Nancy waved at the band, and her drummer began a suspenseful roll. "Nine."

Wayne saw Eugene kissing Virginia back by their table. They turned to watch the stage.

"Eight." The crowd was cheering loudly.

He squeezed Carol and looked up at the platform. It all seemed too right. Too perfect.

"Seven." Fat Nancy turned from the microphone, coughing sharply. She swung back, wiping her mouth with her hand. "Six."

Her voice was hoarse, and Wayne thought Fat Nancy looked confused.

"Five."

The voice was barely a whisper. The hall was suddenly silent.

Fat Nancy dropped the microphone, grabbing at her stomach with both hands and doubling over. She let out a soft, strange whimper, easily heard in the suddenly silent hall. For a moment, everyone froze.

In that split second of inactivity, Fat Nancy toppled forward into her microphone stand and then off the platform, her head hitting the floor with a loud thud. Everyone froze.

A shriek of feedback snapped the dancers back to life, as several men rushed to her side. Wayne was surprised that there were no screams. The crowd was stunned and silent.

Carol turned and buried her face against his shoulder, her hands gripping his back.

Wayne looked between two men, down into Fat Nancy's face. Her neck was twisted oddly from her fall. Her eyes were open, staring emptily at the ceiling. On her mouth Wayne saw a small but definite smile. He stared at it, not understanding.

Then two paramedics from the firehouse reached her and blocked his view.

"She's dead," said the guitarist from the stage. "Jesus Christ. Fat Nancy's dead."

The Gander Girls hugged as a group.

The crowd backed slowly away, then started toward the doors as one of the paramedics shook his head.

Slowly, the people left for home, stunned. If they spoke at all, it was in whispers.

In the car, Virginia was the first to speak. "I've never seen any-one die before." She sat apart from Eugene, bundled against the cold.

"I did once," Carol said. "When I was nine, our minister died in church. He was praying and just never got up." She shivered and leaned into Wayne.

"Why did it have to happen?" Eugene was drunk, tears rolling down his cheeks.

They rode in silence then. The snow kept falling in big, fragile flakes as the old car headed away from the party. In the backseat Wayne kept his arm around Carol, who was crying.

They were a half mile from Virginia's farm when Eugene's car hit a patch of ice. He grunted, jerking the wheel desperately, but the car slid halfway into the ditch.

Eugene tried to back the car onto the road, but the wheels spun uselessly on the ice. Finally he shifted into park and shook his head.

"Shoot, only one thing to do," he said. "I'll hike up the road for help. You all stay here and keep warm." He opened his door.

"Wait up," Virginia said. "If they're still up at Hudson's, you won't be able to get in. I'll come with you." She turned to the back seat. "Watch for our tractor. We won't be long. Our farm is just up on the right."

Then the doors slammed and she and Eugene were gone, crunching off into the dark.

"Just hold me," Carol said. "Why did our one night together have to fall apart? It was all so perfect. It just isn't fair."

"I don't know," he said. "But we're together now." He pulled her closer in the dark.

He kissed her forehead and then her lips as she raised her head. He kissed her again and she kissed back, her fingers on the back of his neck, pulling him closer. He slipped his hands inside her coat, recalling August evenings as they slid downwards on the seat.

But tonight there was no sense of gentle, playful romance in their touching. Tonight, tugging her wool slacks down, he felt only an urgency, a need, and he knew from her nails on his back under his coat that Carol shared this with him. His lips felt bruised as he fumbled with his own pants, then moved to her.

"Wayne," she said into his ear, twisting slightly.

"Yes," he said, stroking, excited. Carol shook her head, but he felt her relax, felt her desire, and pushed into her. Carol whimpered under him, but made no move to resist. Through his shirt, her nails dug into his back. Their breathing fogged the cold car windows.

It was not lovemaking, the way their bodies contorted and twisted together, their eyes shut, faces tense. It was the ultimate act of desire, perhaps, but tonight it was simple and mindless.

Then it was over as Wayne realized what he had forced on them. Barely able to see Carol's face in the dark car, he could sense the utter sadness he had caused. As his desire was replaced by the sharing of that sadness and fresh shame, he realized that in his love for Carol he had failed them both.

Slowly he moved away from her and sat up, trying to understand his actions, his sudden need, and his new, lasting sadness.

"Why?" Carol said softly. "We agreed to wait."

He felt her eyes through the darkness. There was no answer he could give her.

A pair of headlights in the distance flashed on the windows, revealing her tears as she fastened her slacks.

"I do love you," he said, certain only of that. He wanted to hold her, but she slid away on the seat.

The tractor came closer, chattering down the snowy road.

"No you don't," Carol said, zipping her coat, "or you would have stopped." She stepped out of the car and stood beside the ditch.

Wayne opened his door and jumped out into the snow, nearly falling, holding onto the door for support. She turned from the headlights to look at him. No longer was she the sensuous, smiling vision he had treasured but sad, with no light in her eyes for him.

"Don't hate me, Carol. I'm sorry."

"I don't hate you, Wayne," she said, her voice unsteady. "I'm hurt and confused and just as much to blame as you are, I guess."

Her eyes finally met his. "But the trust I had is gone, and I need to think about everything for a while."

"You're lucky you got this far," Virginia's father called from the tractor. "This road is a mess."

Eugene climbed down and connected a chain to the car. He nodded to his father.

"Stand clear, now," Virginia's father yelled.

They backed away as the tractor roared. It had chains on its large wheels, and as they spun before catching, sparks flew up into the snow. Then the car moved slowly back onto the roadway.

Wayne helped Eugene unfasten the chain.

"You boys get home before this gets any worse," the man shouted. "You'll never make it up the mountain. I'll take Carol up to the camp lodge."

She glanced briefly at Wayne, then climbed up onto the tractor, sitting next to Virginia's father in the covered cab. He backed the tractor around, and it chuttered up the road.

"Shoot," said Eugene. "What a way to start the new year. Climb in."

They got in the car, and he started carefully for town, driving in the middle of the road. "What happened with you two? We were gone a long time."

"Nothing," Wayne said. "Nothing happened."

"Well," Eugene said, turning on the radio. "Can't expect much, what with Fat Nancy and all. Tonight was just a total mess."

He couldn't find a station and switched the radio off. "She really screwed tonight up, poor thing."

They rode in silence until Eugene pulled up in front of Wayne's house.

"Good night," he said. "Remember, you can see her tomorrow before she goes home."

"Yeah," Wayne said, stepping into the snow. "Tomorrow's another day. Good night, buddy."

He watched the car fishtail into the street and drive away, silenced by the snow.

Quietly, so as not to wake his family, he went into the house and climbed the bare, squeaky wooden stairs. In his room he saw a sheet of notebook paper on his bed, a reminder from his mother. He wanted to tell her everything, but didn't.

After taking off his shoes, he crept down the hallway to his parents' room and slipped the paper under their door. That way his mother, turning in her bed, could glance and know he was safely home.

He crept back to his room and undressed.

Lying awake with a deep, gutty loneliness, Wayne tried to understand what had happened. He saw a link between Fat Nancy's death and the few, panting moments he and Carol had spent trying to atone for their feeling of emptiness. Slowly, that link grew firmer as its dimensions unfurled for him. He began to understand.

He had reacted to Nancy's death by uniting with a woman, the only act that could ultimately save him from cold oblivion. But in that very act of life is a search for oblivion just as profound. Wayne saw that, in avoiding the reality of death, he had courted its utter peace, that life's very source is founded on the search for death.

Alone in the double bed that nearly filled his small, cold room, Wayne saw for an instant what it would take him years to fully grasp, but which he knew already some could never see.

And as the last snow settled down in the Cape Breton night, he thought of Carol and began to cry.

James O. Weeks

Acknowledgements

Three organizations have given my life strength and value:

1. The Engine Room crew from Fire Company 65, Pennsburg, Pennsylvania. The brave members of this group taught me the importance of trust, service, and friendship.
2. The dedicated nurses of the V.O.N. have restored my health numerous times. I value and respect their selfless service.
3. The Knot Wise Guys meet weekly to solve national and local issues of importance. We seem to have little effect, but the lunches are always enjoyable.

James O. Weeks

About the author

James O. Weeks taught English in secondary schools and community college for forty years. He published articles in professional journals and short genre fiction (*Wilderness Tales*) while teaching young adults about writing. One of his short stories appears in Moose House's second collection of short fiction, *Blink and You'll Miss It;* and Moose House published his first novel, *Nodding's People.*

Beyond the classroom, Jim worked as a swimming pool manager, camp counsellor, and liquor store clerk, and for twelve years was a driver and pump operator for a volunteer fire department.

Jim and his wife (a fifth-generation Nova Scotian) live in Lunenburg.